NUBB TROUBLE

A Teddy and Pip Story

By Lisa Maddock

© 2013 Lisa Maddock
All Rights Reserved

No part of this publication may be reproduced, stored in a retrieval system, or transmitted, in any form, by any means, electronic, mechanical, photocopying, recording, or otherwise, without permission of the author.

First published by Cavidae Press
Shakopee, Minnesota 55379

ISBN: 978-0615927428

This book is printed on acid-free paper.
This book is a work of fiction. Places, events, and situations in this book are purely fictional and any resemblance to actual persons, living or dead, is coincidental.

Printed in the United States of America.

Thank you to Allison Maddock, a fantastically meticulous copyeditor who loves guinea pigs and good grammar.

Nubb Trouble is dedicated to all of Teddy and Pip's fans and friends! YOU are the best of times!

Also by Lisa Maddock

Teddy and Pip:

A Tale of Two Guinea Pigs
The Bridezilla Who Stole Christmas
The Trouble With Max

The Lucy Mackensie Series (age 12 and up):

Silver Linings Part One

PROLOGUE

Notes: The Case of the Haunted House

This is what Daddy said: usually people do mean things because they have had mean things done to them first. He said this rule is even about our neighborhood bully, Benny Nubb.

Instead of only trying to get proof that Benny Nubb is the bad guy in my latest mystery, he thinks I should try to understand him. Daddy even said (get ready for this) that maybe at the end of this case, Benny Nubb and I might end up as friends.

I hate to say it, but I think my dad is wrong or even a little bit cuckoo on this one.

But I am a good detective and turn over every possible rock and stone in my cases, even really small ones. So I will try to understand that boy.

I did some asking around, and this is what I found out about Benny Nubb (who I will now call "BN") so far: He is a fifth grader (I already knew that) and has lived in the house next door to Wally and Amelia for as long as I have lived where I live (I already knew that, too). Maybe even longer — maybe his whole entire life. Before Wally fixed it up and he and Amelia became Nubb neighbors, BN lived next door to an empty haunted house. Maybe living next door to a haunted house makes a person cuckoo, or a bully. I will do more research on that if I can find the time.

    The suspect, BN, has a mom and a dad, plus two big brothers (I don't know their names, but people say that they are bullies, too). The Nubb family has a big black dog named Rufus (who needs some obedience school, if you ask me).

    Weirdly enough, BN has a lot of friends (all boys). At lunch, those boys clump around him and laugh at his mean stuff. His mean stuff includes throwing peas at girls and stealing smaller kids' desserts. I have seen him trip people and knock books out of kids' hands, too. BN is a mean teaser who thinks his teasing is really funny. He could not be more wrong; it is not one bit funny.

    On the bus, he teases little kids and even pushes them out of seats so he can sit there instead. He also opens bus windows when he isn't supposed to, which makes the bus driver really grouchy. BN is the kind of kid who puts gum on the back of seats and other icky places. Around our neighborhood, besides scaring guinea pigs, he likes to zoom around on his bike (sometimes on the sidewalk). He goes so fast that he could knock over a grandma or make a dog run right into the street. He laughs while he does that stuff.

    I won't say "case closed" on this one, even though the circumstantial evidence is really, really strong against him. Here it is: He was in Amelia's yard on Monday before the noises started up. He has opportunity (he lives next door). And motive? Meanness. He is the meanest boy around, by far.

I am a fair detective and try to be a fair person, so I will keep working to get evidence. Even though it is really hard, and I am getting nowhere. But no evidence means no accusing. Innocent until proven guilty. That is the rule of law.

But no accusing also means he won't stop. Not stopping means more bad days and nights for Amelia, Teddy and Pip.

And Daddy, sorry, but I think the chances of that boy and me ending up friends is about one percent. One penny out of a whole dollar. Or if there was some money smaller than a penny, that'd be the chance.

Signed,
Molly Jane Fisher
Detective

Chapter One
A quick surveillance oughta do the trick

Wednesday night, Hannah, Nora and I knelt at Hannah's bedroom window with all of our eyes on Benny Nubb's house. So far, nothing had happened. It was the only time ever that I wished that boy would *do* something.

We had been watching for a while — not the zillion hours that it felt like, but a long time — and my crime-fighting partners were getting silly. Hannah was having a giggle fit like she sometimes does, even when things are totally serious. Nora, who was finally done being mad at me for the day, was catching those giggles from Hannah.

I understood why they were doing that. I mean, it was boring and tense, and Hannah has a very catchy giggle. I sure didn't want to be the grouchy one in the group, the one telling them to be serious or quiet. My friends were totally helping me out, and it was my case and responsibility, after all. So I kept my mouth quiet and my eyes on the boring Nubb house.

Yep, Benny Nubb lives across the street from my friend Hannah Brady. For today, it was convenient for the case, but too bad for Hannah every other day of her whole life! This was my surveillance. I had thought it would be enough to wrap up the case. Easy as pie, or cake, or whatever. Except that nothing was happening. I guess it had been too easy, too perfect. I hadn't even had to tell any not-quite-truths to get myself into the perfect spying spot tonight; if anyone asked, Hannah, Nora and I *were* working on our State Fair projects . . . just not at that exact moment.

You want to know what a State Fair project is, right? Hang on, you'll know soon enough. I can hardly get away from that thing for ten whole seconds these days, so it'll come up again soon.

So, anyway, about the surveillance. Hannah borrowed binoculars and her family's fancy camera. The camera is just as good for surveillance as looking through binoculars is — maybe even better. I told Hannah she could use the camera instead of me. The binoculars seemed like a cheaper option to be responsible for in case something broke.

Nora didn't have anything to do surveillance with except her eyeballs. At first, that was a problem and made her grumpy. Or grumpier. She was already grumpy at me because she really wanted me to come to her house tonight to work on the project. And also to play with Peanut and her new guinea pig, Coco Butter (Coco for short). I love Nora's guinea pigs and going to her house. Believe me, I do. But I had a case to solve all of a sudden, so plans had to change.

It seems like forever since Nora and I were just best friends and not State Fair partners. I miss being best friends. Working on the project for weeks and weeks is starting to mean little bitty fights between us are happening more and more. Not terrible fights, only little ones. But it's like having a bunch of itchy bug bites. After a while, lots of bug bites drive you just as cuckoo as something like a scraped-up knee. Know what I mean?

Lucky for us, the fair is on Friday and it will finally all be over. We can do our perfect presentation for the parents and judges, win the purple grand prize ribbon, then get back to what we really love: guinea pigs.

"Someone's coming!" Hannah squeaked.

"Molly?! Someone's coming!"

Finally, some action! I aimed the binoculars at the front door, then at the garage, where I saw someone coming out of the house. "You guys? Shhh! Please? I can hardly concentrate here."

Nora and Hannah kept on giggling through their hands as I adjusted the binoculars. Darn. Whoever had come out of the house was too tall to be Benny Nubb. Another person came out. He was also too tall to be Benny Nubb. He hollered something back at the house, or at someone in the house, then headed toward a junky car in the driveway. The first guy followed him.

"Those are his big brothers," Nora whispered.

"Oh," I whispered back.

"They're mean too," Nora added. "One time —"

"That's him, that's him, that's him!" Hannah whispered this in a really loud whisper. "Molly! Benny Nubb!" Then the giggles started all over again.

I found Benny Nubb in the binoculars. "Shh!" I said to my two friends again. "You guys, this is it! Help me watch! Hannah, get the camera ready. Please," I added real quick so I wouldn't sound bossy.

Nora pressed her face against the window and Hannah adjusted the camera.

The tall boys turned, because Benny Nubb was talking to them. No, not talking to them. Yelling at them. He was yelling so loud that I could hear what he was saying right through the closed upstairs window.

"Give it back, you stupid jerks!"

Whoa. If I talked to someone in my family like that, I would be in trouble. I mean, I never would even think of doing it — no way — but I guess the Nubbs are used to that kind of talk. One of his brothers started laughing. And then he held something high over his head. I zoomed in on what looked like a stack of papers.

"What are they doing?" Nora whispered.

"Teasing," Hannah said.

I have to be honest, it was weird to see Benny Nubb getting teased by two bigger boys. I was surprised to find myself feeling the littlest bit sorry for him.

Good grief. Now the three boys were pushing and tackling each other in the grass. The big brothers seemed to be having a fun time, but Benny Nubb was yelling his head off. I guessed that a parent or two would come out of that house at any second.

"Isn't somebody going to stop them?" Nora whispered.

"Give them one more second . . ." I said.

The front door opened exactly one second after I said that, making all three of us squeak with surprise. Nora and Hannah started giggling again. "Good one, Molly!" they both said.

Nubb Trouble

The mom stepped out of the house with her arms crossed.

"Mrs. Nubb," Hannah told us.

Even from across the street and high up, I could tell that she was pretty mad. I could also tell that she was not shocked, but used to this. "Will you three *knock it off*?!" she hollered.

There was more hollering after that. I think it was Benny, explaining that it wasn't his fault, that he didn't do anything. And then the papers they had all been wrestling over got dropped and went fluttering down to the grass. "What in the name of Pete?!" Mrs. Nubb hollered. "Stop that! Curtis! Doug! I mean it! That's your brother's homework!"

They knocked it off, but when they were not looking, Benny took a leap and tackled one of his brothers right to the ground.

Nora groaned, "Holy moly. Why did he do that?"

"He wouldn't have if his mom wasn't there to protect him," Hannah said.

The mom yelled some more, then tugged Benny off of his brother.

"It must be tough being the mom of three Nubbs," I said, which made my friends start up their giggling again.

"Stop it! All of you!" Mrs. Nubb yelled at her sons. Then she quieted down and pointed here and there until all of her kids were standing up straight. "Benny? Get your stuff and go inside."

Benny Nubb gathered up his papers and stomped away without saying anything to his mom. The door slammed really loud.

"You two?" Mrs. Nubb shook her head. "Stay out of trouble, or that car is going nowhere this weekend. I mean it!"

The Nubb brothers got in the noisy, junky car and left.

The three of us stayed by the window, thinking and stuff, until Hannah's brother banged on the door.

"Hannah! Did you steal my binoculars?" he shouted.

I shoved the binoculars at Hannah, feeling guilty all the way down to my toenails.

"Go away!" Hannah shouted back.

"Well, did you?" he called, banging some more on the door. "I'm telling Mom if you did!"

"I . . . am not using your binoculars!" Hannah shouted through the closed door, as she carefully set them on the floor. (That is called finding a fast loophole.)

"What's the problem here? Hannah?" Hannah's mom knocked on the door and we all scrambled away from the window.

Hannah unlocked her door and flicked on a light with lightning speed so when her mom peeked in we weren't doing anything.

"Hi, Mom," she said. "What's up?"

"Have you seen Jordan's binoculars?"

Hannah did a shrug as her mom's eyes scanned the room. She slowly left.

As soon as the door was closed again, we all fell onto Hannah's bed, giggling our heads off. Yep, even me. Because sometimes you just have to, to get rid of the stress.

Whew.

Chapter Two
Sleepless night number three

Lying on her side in the soft light of a small corner lamp, Amelia Dearling gazed down at her two amazing, furry little friends. Two sets of wide black eyes looked up at her, small warm bodies pressed against her. The guinea pigs had long since left the cozy cuddle cup intended for them to sleep in. Both were now pressed against the elbow propping up Amelia's weary head. Her eyelids fluttered. She was so tired.

This made night number three, and she was not sure that she could make it through. In spite of the tiredness, she reached out a comforting hand and stroked one guinea pig, then the other. "It's alright. Go to sleep, darlings," she whispered. "Everything is alright." Oh no. There was the sound again.

TAP TAP TAP . . . TAP TAP TAP!
TAP TAP TAP . . . TAP TAP TAP!

Teddy squeaked, "*Amelia!*" and pressed even closer.

"Shh, it's alright," Amelia murmured again. "It's alright. Nothing will hurt you. I am right here. Shh. . . ."

"*IT IS NOT ALRIGHT!*" Pip shrieked in his squeaky little scream. "*MONSTERS ARE TAPPING AND TAPPING AND TAPPING! MONSTERS, AMELIA! AND MONSTERS ARE NOT ALRIGHT! HOW CAN YOU SAY THAT MONSTERS ARE ALRIGHT?! HOW CAN YOU SAY THAT THING TO US?!*"

"No," she murmured. "No monsters, sweetheart. It's only a noise. It's something else. Not monsters, silly. Go to sleep."

"*YES! YES! YES, SILLY! THIS IS NOT THE TIME FOR JOKES! MONSTERS WANT TO COME IN! THEY WANT TO EAT US ALL UP! THEY DO! THEY DO!*"

"Darling Pippen, there are no monsters in Westerfield, New Jersey. Of that, I am certain. And absolutely no one wishes to harm you, or me. We are perfectly safe, my loves. Go to sleep now."

It was not a good sign when Teddy, usually the more reasonable of the pair, agreed with Pip. "*Amelia, I am sorry to call you wrong, but you are this time about this thing. Before, maybe there were no monsters in Westerfield. But now there surely are! It is a monster tap-tap-tapping with clickety-click fingers,*" Teddy whispered, "*Maybe more than one monster. Maybe there are seventeen monsters!*"

"No," Amelia whispered.

"*Floaty ghost monsters who can only tap, but if they tap and tap, day after day after day, then they will get inside this very house! And maybe Pip is right and they will surely eat us all up!*"

Amelia again said, "No. Teddy, my darling, I promise that seventeen monsters are not tapping on our windows."

"*Are you saying to me that there are MORE monsters?!*" Teddy squeaked.

"No, of course not."

"MONSTERS WANT US OUT OF THIS HOUSE, AMELIA! MAD, TAPPING, CLICKETY MONSTERS! THAT IS WHAT THEY WANT!"

Tap tap tap . . . tap tap tap . . . tap tap tap. . . .

Of course Amelia Dearling did not believe in monsters with clicking fingers or otherwise, but — what in the world *was* making those tapping noises? There had been no such sounds before she had left on her trip. And Max had not mentioned anything after spending the weekend here with Teddy and Pip.

Or had he?

No. If he had, she would have remembered such a thing.

But still. Perhaps she should give Max a call.

But, good heavens, not now! It was the middle of the night. Exhaustion was making her forget things.

She had first noticed the noises Monday night after she had returned from the trip. At first, she had thought it was a tree branch hitting the window, but there were no trees near the front of the house. None with branches long enough to tap like that, anyway. And, besides, it was not especially windy. What would make a sound like that, and why would it begin so suddenly and then go on and on so regularly?

Perhaps Dan Fisher could stop by tomorrow and take a look around. Yes, she would call Dan. Molly's father would know about such things.

Tap tap tap . . . tap tap tap . . . tap tap tap. . . .

On the other hand, there was that boy next door. What was his name? The boy had been in the yard on Monday. She had seen him for sure, caught his guilty look before he darted off with his big black dog.

TAP TAP TAP . . . TAP TAP TAP!
TAP TAP TAP . . . TAP TAP TAP!

Guinea pig noses pressed against her as her thoughts continued. But goodness, it was so very late for a boy of that age to be out causing mischief. Amelia yawned. Didn't parents of young boys keep an eye on them and make sure that they were tucked in their beds?

Benny. That was the name. Molly was looking into the possibility that Benny was the cause of all of this exhaustion and anxiety. But poor Molly was so very busy with her school project — her State Fair. Jane had mentioned this to her when they spoke that evening. Molly had precious little time to be sleuthing in addition to her school work.

Amelia lost her train of thought and fought to get it back. Oh yes, the neighbor boy. Well, she certainly did not want to have a talk with the boy's mother without solid proof of her son's wrongdoing, and she did not have proof. She felt certain that accusing a boy of wrongdoing without proof would hurt neighborly relationships. And she and Wally wanted only to live a quiet, private life here on Taylor Drive, not one full of conflict or awkwardness. Or exhaustion. Or anxiety.

TAP TAP TAP . . . TAP TAP TAP!

Or tapping noises in the night.

The truth was that this was a puzzle she felt incapable of solving after so little sleep. And it did not help that Teddy and Pip were creating more and more difficult-to-deal-with explanations and scenarios all the time.

Apparently the tapping sounds had now become monsters with clicking fingers. Where in the world did they come up with thoughts like that? Perhaps it was time to take away that television set.

Oh, how she wished Wally were here. Wally, with his smooth, quiet, calm, rational ways.

"Darlings, I simply must get some sleep," Amelia murmured as she felt a nose pushing against her hand. "We will figure this out in the morning. We will. I promise. Now sleep. Please."

"*Amelia, there is no need for figuring. We have it figured, Pip and me. We need to move away from this haunted house. Now or sooner. That is the figure. So, let's go. Okay? Please?*"

"THIS HOUSE IS NO GOOD! WE NEED TO GET OUT!" Pip said, and then lowered his voice to a whisper to sing a little song.

Tap tap tap! I hear it and dread.
Tap-ping scares me out of my head!
Tap tap tap! It comes in the night.
Tap tap tap! It gives us a fright!
Tap tap, clickety fingers, I say.
The tapping is monsters and we need to move away!

Teddy said, "*Amelia, excuse me, but Pip is right on this one, for a change. We need to go back to* the safe place of Molly Jane's house, now or sooner. Please? Let's go, okay? Okay?"

TAP TAP TAP . . . TAP TAP TAP!
TAP TAP TAP . . . TAP TAP TAP!
TAP TAP TAP . . . TAP TAP TAP!
Tap tap tap . . . tap tap tap . . . tap tap tap. . . .
"Amelia!"
"AMELIA!"

"Boys, noises cannot hurt you. We covered this territory last night."

"*Monsters can hurt you,*" Teddy whispered. "*Monsters make the noises, Amelia. That is the newest carrot-ory.*"

"*Territory,* darling," Amelia corrected softly. "Boys, couldn't we all simply think happy thoughts and get through this night? Wally will be back on Friday night. Only two more nights. . . ." Her voice drifted off as the impossibility of getting through two more nights occurred to her. "When Wally is back, everything will be back to normal, darlings."

"*No! Surely that is not true, Amelia! Wally is who these monsters are clicking for!*"

Amelia opened her eyes. "What did you say, Teddy?"

"*Amelia, these clicking monsters are mad because Wally hammered and sawed them out of their house. That is the problem here. That is the carrot-ory.*"

Amelia's mouth dropped open. She could think of absolutely nothing to say in response to that.

"*Monsters are doing the revenge, Amelia. That is what the tap-tap-tapping is all about, and so Wally is in much more danger than even we are! We must* go to a safer place sooner than later! It is already too much later, I think!"

Pip pushed at her hand repeatedly. "*WE NEED TO PACK THE BOXES! LET'S GO! LET'S GO!*" Push, push, push, push.

Amelia moved the hand carefully out of Pip's way, then reached out to stroke Teddy's fur. "It's two o'clock in the morning, darlings," she finally murmured.

"*Monsters do not wear watches,*" Teddy pointed out. "*They do not care if it is the time of two or three or four —*"

"*DARKLY MORNING IS MONSTER TIME, AMELIA! IT IS THEIR FAVORITE TIME TO TAP AND CLICK! TWO O'CLOCK IS A GOOD TIME FOR THEM!*"

Amelia rolled onto her back and covered her face with both hands. Whether on the brink of laughing or crying, she wasn't sure.

"*Amelia! Are you alright?*" Teddy squeaked, then gave her a little push with his nose.

"*AMELIA! DO NOT FALL TO PIECES ON US! DO NOT FREAK OUT!*"

She could feel them closing in on her, whiskers now tickling her cheek. "I am alright, my dears," she finally said, turning back on her side to face them. "Not falling apart. Not freaking out. But darlings, I am ever so exhausted."

"*We are sorry, best friend Amelia, but . . . but we are also so very afraid,*" Teddy whispered as he and Pip crowded as close to her as possible. "*We do not know what to do if we are far from you. We are scared out of our little heads now, and you are our only hope."*

"It is alright," she soothed them. "We will stay together. We will make it through this night together."

"*Together is what we need. We like the together very much,*" Teddy said. "*And then tomorrow, we will move away from this haunted house. The end. Hooray!*"

Amelia murmured, "No, we will not be moving away. We cannot simply leave. Not this house, our house."

"*Monsters, Amelia,*" Teddy groaned.

"IF WE STAY IN THIS PLACE, TOMORROW WE WILL BE CRUNCHY-CRUNCH MONSTER FOOD! CRUNCH CRUNCH, AMELIA! CRUNCH CRUNCH!"

"Boys, I hesitate to mention this, but I have reason to believe that the noises are being made by our neighbor boy, Benny Nubb," Amelia said.

"*Amelia, nice try, but these noises are not made by the neighbor boy of Nubb. The sounds are not made by human boy fingers. I am sure of it.*"

"NEIGHBOR BOYS CALLED NUBB DO NOT HAVE CLICKETY FINGERS, AMELIA! BUT GOOD JOB ANYWAY!"

"*Boys have stub fingers, not clickety ones. Nubb stub fingers.*"

"NUBB NUBB NUBB! STUB STUB STUB!"

"*Tee hee!*"

"IT IS NOT NUBB! THE END!"

"Oh, alright, boys. Okay." Amelia yawned, then hummed a tune and stroked soft fur. The humming turned to soft singing about sleep and sweet dreams.

But eyes stayed open as the clock ticked and the night went on.

"TELL US A STORY!" Pip squeaked. "*MAKE IT A GOOD ONE WHERE PIP SAVES THE DAY! A STORY WITH NO MONSTERS. PLEASE AND THANK YOU!*"

"A good one where Pip saves the day, hmm?" Amelia smiled. "Alright. How about a story about two brave castle knights named Sir Theodore and Sir Pippen —"

"*OBJECTION! OBJECTION! WHY ALWAYS IS TEDDY GOING FIRST ON THE LIST OF BRAVE KNIGHTS AND ALSO ALL OTHER LISTS?*"

The story was told, the ending was happy, "good nights" were said, and, just like the past two nights, exhaustion took over and Amelia fell asleep.

But the tapping did not stop, and Teddy and Pip did not sleep.

"*Molly Jane, too, is thinking that the clickety tapping is the work of this neighbor boy of Nubb, but we will make her believe the truth. Then she will help us to pack the boxes and move away from here,*" Teddy said.

"*MOLLY JANE WILL SAVE THE DAY! I WILL SING OF IT IN MY NEWEST HIT SINGLE,*" Pip said.

If a day needs saving,
Molly Jane will do it!
If a day needs saving,
She is the one!
If a day needs saving,
Molly Jane will do it!

As soon as we see . . . the sun!

"Yes, Pip, that is what will happen. We will not have to have one more night of afraid and worry after this no-good one we are in."

TAP TAP TAP. . . .

Crunch crunch crunch. . . .

"CRUNCHING! TEDDY! NOW THERE IS CRUNCHING! DO YOU HEAR THAT THING?! HOW IS IT THAT FLOATY MONSTERS HAVE CRUNCHY-CRUNCH FEET?!"

"Yes, Pip, I hear the crunching but do not know how monsters can both click and crunch. Do not wake Amelia for now. I will be the guard first, then you can do your turn. Just like we did other nights. If you are not going to do sleeping, please do not do loud singing for now. Thank you." Teddy rested his head on front paws and sighed. It was going to be another long night.

Chapter Three
Tweets's clue

TAP! Tap tap tap.
TAP! Tap tap tap.
"The letter B?" I asked. "Is that right, Tweets?"
TAP! Tap tap tap.
I took another bite of cereal and crunched. One long, then three short. Yep, he was tapping out the letter B on the window.
TAP! Tap tap tap.
"Okay, Tweets, I've got it! B! What's next?"
"Pretty boy! Pretty, pretty, pretty! Birdie!"
Tweets, my green and yellow parakeet, can say words all of a sudden (cool, huh?), and I think he is sending me a message using Morse code.

You think I'm crazy for thinking that, don't you? Well, let me ask you one thing: have you read the other stories about me, Teddy and Pip? If you have, then you will understand why I think it is possible for a parakeet to know and use Morse code. In fact, I don't think it will seem crazy to you at all.

Tweets started talking on Monday, after we got back from Florida. Or maybe he started while we were gone. I can't be sure. Anyway, he started the window-tapping last night, always on the window that faces Teddy and Pip's house. Teddy and Pip's house is two houses down, but Tweets has that great birdie-vision. Normally he likes to try out different window sills, but all of a sudden, only that one will do. It can't be a coincidence! He is trying to tell me something, and I believe it is through Morse code.

TAP! Tap tap tap.

"I've got it, Tweets. B. Now give me the next letter, please," I said again.

Besides this tapping, Tweets's talk has mostly been about himself and how pretty he is. He *is* pretty, don't get me wrong. But it would be nice if he mentioned . . . you know . . . *me*, once in a while.

TAP! Tap tap tap.

Apparently I was only going to get B this morning. Or ever. But maybe that was all I needed. B for Benny Nubb, of course. I thought for a while, doodling Benny Nubb's name on my piece of paper. I mean, Morse code is a lot of work, and Tweets is just a little bird. So he picked the letter used first and last to give me the clue.

"Tweets, you are a genius!"

TAP! Tap tap tap.

"I think it's him too. Totally. But we need some evidence."

"Molly, why is that bird on the window again?" Mom called from the sink.

"Tweets," I corrected her. "And he is a total genius!"

Mom was on the phone with Aunt Patty, having a giggly conversation about Max and his (my face scrunched up at the thought of it) *girlfriend*, Sophie.

Thinking about a girlfriend for Max always made me feel really scrunchy. I actually do not believe that Max has a girlfriend. Not a real one; not like that. He is much too cool for that.

"How adorable! Well, I will have to invite Max and Sophie over for dinner sometime soon," Mom said, then giggled some more. "Are they free Saturday night?"

Good grief. Mom? Giggling?

"Molly? The bird needs to get back in the cage — almost time for the bus," she said, moving the phone away from her mouth. "You need to finish your breakfast!"

My mom can think about and do seventeen things all at one time. That is pretty cool, except when sixteen of them are related to locking Tweets up and stopping me from working on my case.

Tweets lives in the kitchen now. Since he's started to talk, he kind of wakes me up in the morning super early, talking about himself. But if he's in the kitchen, we can all enjoy him — not only me — and nobody loses any sleep.

"*Hello!*"

"Hi, Tweets! It's a B, right? I'm not getting that wrong, am I?"

Tweets bobbed his head up and down, up and down, his eyes getting crazy.

"Is that a 'yes,' or are you just being wound up?"

Bob bob bob bob bob. . . .

"What does that mean?" I asked. It is a lot harder to figure out what Tweets is saying than what Teddy and Pip are saying. See, Teddy and Pip, my two favorite guinea pigs, can actually talk. Yes, I said talk, and I mean more than a few copied words. Pip can sing, too. If you haven't read my other stories, try to do that; it is amazing stuff. I wish I had time to explain it now, but I have to go to school.

TAP! Tap tap tap. "*Pretty, pretty, pretty bird! Pretty birdie!*"

I crunched up a spoonful of Cheerios. "Yes, Tweets, you are a pretty bird. Want some cereal?"

"Swallow first, Molly. Don't give him cereal!" Mom used the eyes in the back of her head for that one.

"*Pretty boy!*" *Bob bob bob.* . . .

"He wants some! Look at him! Can't I give him a little treat?"

"Sugar is not good for him, Molly — bye, Patty. talk to you later." Mom finally put the phone down. "If he wants a treat, he can have some . . . some . . . broccoli."

"Broccoli?" I shook my head.

"But he really needs to get back inside, Molly. The bus. . . ."

"It's actually not coming for ten more minutes," I said. "Where's Daddy? His eggs are getting all yucky." I gave the eggs a careful poke with my finger.

"He went to Amelia's house earlier this morning," Mom said as she inspected the window sill for bird poop.

"Why?" I frowned just a bitty bit. It sounded to me like maybe Daddy was working on my case, and I didn't feel good about that.

"When he got back, he disappeared right into his office," Mom went on. She looked at the closed office door, then at the eggs. "I suppose I'll pop them in the microwave."

"*Hello!*" Tweets chirped. *TAP! Tap tap tap.*

Mom stopped with Daddy's plate in her hand. "Every time that bird is out, he flies right to *that* window and bumps his beak against it."

"I noticed that too," I said. "I think he's. . . ." I quickly shoved cereal into my mouth and started to chew. My mom is not a person who likes to hear or think much about amazing stuff. It makes her nervous or freaked out for some reason. She still cannot handle the whole "Teddy and Pip can talk" thing after almost a whole year. I smartly decided not to share my case-solving Morse code information with her.

"*Hello! Hello! Hello!*"

"Hello, bird."

"*Hello!*"

"Do you still want to come along to see Nanna tomorrow afternoon, after the State Fair?" Mom asked.

"*Pretty boy! Pretty birdie!*" *TAP! Tap tap tap.*

"Yes, Tweets, you are beautiful," I said.

"Molly?" Mom snapped her fingers at me.

"Huh?"

"Nanna? Tomorrow?"

"Yes, I want to see Nanna. Of course I do. Rats. Oh, darn it!"

"What?" Mom had gone back to doing lots of things at once. The microwave started doing its buzzy work on Daddy's breakfast.

"I owe every one of my grandmas pictures and letters! I haven't started a single one, Mom! When am I going to have time to do that?" My insides started to feel tight on me as I remembered how much stuff I had to do.

"I'll help you tonight," Mom said as she pulled the plate out of the microwave and gave the eggs her own little poke. "Don't worry."

"Thanks, Mom! You're the best!"

"*Pretty, pretty, pretty, pretty boy!*" Tweets decided to move to the place Mom likes him to be least of all (except for on top of her head): the ceiling fan. That was the end of his freedom. (Tweets does not always show good judgment.)

Mom pointed at his cage.

I climbed up on the table, collected him from off of the ceiling fan (something I am getting really speedy at), climbed back down, then swooped him back in.

"*Come in, Molly Jane Fisher! Over and over! Come in! Come in, Molly Jane!*" came a voice from somewhere in the house.

Mom and I looked at each other.

"*Come in, Molly Jane Fisher! Come in Molly Jane! Where are you?! Roger? Over?*"

"Teddy?"

Mom made a confused face.

"*MOLLY JANE, COME ON! DO NOT MAKE US MAD! WHERE ARE YOU?! OVER AND OVER!*"

"Pip, are you here too? Where are you guys?"

"*Molly Jane!*"

"*MOLLY JANE!*"

Then Daddy peeked out of the office and grinned a big grin at me. He waved me toward him and said, "Got a minute?"

"Only a minute!" Mom called. "The bus. . . ."

Chapter Four
Video chatting

"Daddy! Oh my gosh!" I said, because Teddy and Pip were talking to me on Daddy's computer screen.

"This is a video chat. They can see you because *this*," Daddy said, pointing to a little circle on top of his computer, "is a camera. Those two are streaming live from down the street." Then he blew his nose, because Daddy is allergic to furry animals.

"Oh my gosh," I breathed. "Cool!"

"*Oh our gosh too, Molly Jane!*"

"*GOSH GOSH GOSH!*"

"Daddy! What a perfect and awesome idea! Thank you!"

My dad laughed a little, then said, "You're welcome," and blew his nose some more. "It was mostly Amelia's idea."

"Dan? Breakfast!" Mom called.

"Have fun!" Daddy blew me a kiss, then blew his nose some more and left the office.

I turned my attention to Teddy and Pip. "You guys are a TV show! You are on my dad's computer screen!" I giggled.

"BEST OF TIMES IS THIS THING! PIP IS A ROCK STAR! LOOK AT ME ROCKING ON DAD'S COMPUTER TV!"

"Teddy, too, is rocking, Molly Jane!"

"Hi, Teddy! Look at you rock!"

"AND MOLLY JANE IS A TV SHOW! MOLLY JANE SQUAREPANTS!"

"Tee hee! Good one, Pip!"

"TEE HEE! TEE HEE!"

"This is a fun and funny time for guinea pigs! I am not remembering a time of good before this one, Molly Jane. It has been a long time."

"I'm so sorry about that, Teddy. How are things going?"

"Pip and me are scared out of our little heads, Molly Jane. That is how it is going."

"Sorry."

"When we are done with the tee hee of this computer talk, we will talk of that. But not for now."

"I am so sorry that you guys are having a hard time. I wish I could —"

"Molly Jane, we know that thing," Teddy said. "We know you are sorry for our troubles. Let us not talk of them just yet."

"MOLLY JANE, DO SPONGEY-BOB DANCES! MAKE YOUR LEGS SQUIGGLY! CAN YOU DO THAT THING? I WANT TO SEE THAT THING, MOLLY JANE SQUAREPANTS! LET'S GO! DANCE! DANCE, MOLLY JANE!" Pip squealed. "TV SHOWS ARE NOT ONLY TALKING. THEY ARE ABOUT DOING FUNNY THINGS! DO FUNNY THINGS!"

"Hello, Molly." Amelia's tired but smiling face popped onto the screen.

"*There's Amelia! We love Amelia! Where have you been, best friend Amelia? Why were you so very far away before this?*"

"*MOLLY JANE, HERE IS ANOTHER TV STAR! IT IS THE PERSON OF AMELIA, WHO WE LOVE, WHO SHOULD NOT BE LEAVING US ALL ALONE LIKE SHE DID JUST NOW!*"

"Hi, Amelia."

"Sorry to intrude on your busy morning, Molly, but I thought perhaps a little diversion might appeal to the boys."

"Amelia, this is awesome — not intruding!"

"We won't keep you. I know you have a bus to catch," she went on.

"*BUSES STINK!*"

"Pip, really!" Amelia said.

"*BUSES ARE YELLOW AND BIG AND SMELLY AND GO BUMPITY-BUMP! THEY ARE MONSTERS THAT EAT KIDS AND ARE WORST OF TIMES!*"

"Pip, buses don't eat kids or smell bad," I said.

"*WRONG!*"

"Have you ever been on one?"

"*MOLLY JANE, DO NOT ARGUE WITH ME! BUSSES ARE P.U.!*"

"How did it go last night?" I asked Amelia.

"I don't want you to worry about it," she said.

That meant it had gone badly.

"I apologize for pulling you into our troubles during such a busy week at school. Had I known about your State Fair, I never would have asked for your help yesterday."

"The State Fair? Don't even worry about that. I have that stuff under control. Besides, I promised I'd solve this problem for you, and I will. I am so close to getting evidence against Benny Nubb. So, so, so close. Please don't give up on me, Amelia!"

"Oh, Molly dear, I am most certainly not giving up on you. No. It's just that. . . ." Amelia sighed. "The noises went on well into the early hours of the morning, and frankly, I am almost too tired to think." She rubbed her forehead a bit.

"The early hours? Do you mean, like, one o'clock in the morning?" I asked Amelia. How could Benny Nubb keep up that kind of mischief for so many hours in a row? How could *anyone*? Gee whiz! How mean *was* he? Didn't he have other things to do?

"Unfortunately, yes, that is what I mean. Off and on, until very late."

I had a bad thought then. Did he have *accomplices*? ("Accomplices" means other people helping to do the crime.) Were his mean brothers helping him, or his tons of friends? Holy moly.

"Amelia? Don't give up hope. I will close this case by tonight. I promise." Whoops. I definitely should not have promised something so specific. A detective can never be that sure of when a case will be closed. It just plain doesn't work that way. But my promise made Amelia look a little bit less tired and more hopeful so I couldn't take it back.

"Thank you, Molly, for everything," she murmured. "You three enjoy each other," she said as she backed away. "Teddy? Pip? No complaints when Molly has to go to school. I will be attempting to do a bit of writing in the kitchen. I will not be far," she added quickly. "Boys, remember your manners."

"AMELIA, YOU SILLY! WE DO NOT NEED MANNERS TO WATCH MOLLY JANE TV!"

"This thing called diversion is much fun," Teddy said. "Molly Jane, we should do this all the day long. We would like that, Pip and me. Molly Jane TV all the day. School should be the thing called 'cancelled' so Molly Jane Fisher can do the diversion. Right, Molly Jane? Do you want to do the cancel and then diversion? Or else Pip can do the cancel for you. Do you want Pip to do that thing? He can do it scary-good."

"PIP CAN DO IT! I WILL CANCEL!" Pip got super close to the camera. "DO SOMETHING, MOLLY JANE! I WANT TO SEE SOMETHING FUNNY! TELL JOKES OR DANCE! WAIT! NO, NO, NO! NEVER MIND THAT THING FOR NOW! MOLLY JANE, LISTEN! YOU NEED TO HEAR MY NEW HIT SINGLE!"

"Okay, honey, but scoot back a little. All I can see is your nose right now!" I laughed. "You are wound up this morning, Pip!"

"NO! YOU ARE THE ONE WHO IS WOUND UP, MOLLY JANE! TEE HEE!"

"Molly Jane, Pip is a springy-spring-spring. That is the kind of wound up he is."

"Back up, Pip, so I don't only see your nose."

"NOSEY-NOSE-NOSE! TEE HEE! I AM ONLY A BIG NOSE NOW! NOSE TV! THIS IS NOSEY-NOSE-NOSE TV NOW!"

"Pip, back up so Molly Jane does not only see your big nosey-nose," Teddy said. "She does not want to see that thing! Nobody wants to only see that thing on the TV!"

Pip backed up, but only a little. Then he yelled, "NO MORE WORDS ABOUT NOSES! THIS IS NOT THE TIME TO TALK ABOUT NOSES! LATER I WILL WRITE A SONG ABOUT THOSE FUNNY THINGS, BUT NOT NOW! LISTEN TO THE HIT SINGLE." Pip did a little throat-clear.

Haunted houses stink.
It's not like you think.
Scared to take a drink,
Or be too close to the sink.
Haunted . . . houses . . . STINK!

Pip ended his song close up to the camera. "THIS IS NOT A JOKE SONG, MOLLY JANE! HAUNTED HOUSES ARE NOT FUNNY!"

Teddy pushed his way to the camera in front of Pip and said, "*Molly Jane, like you heard just now from Pip's song, our house that was a perfect one before is now a haunted one full of bad times that go on and on. Pip is right. It is not funny. This is called serious business. That is the carrot-ory.*"

"The . . . what?"

"CARROT-ORY! THE CARROT-ORY, MOLLY JANE!"

"Look, guys, maybe there were stories about that house being haunted before Wally fixed it up, but now —"

"*Molly Jane, we must pack the boxes and move back to the house that Dad Dan built. It is not* safe here in this one. It is not our Wally's fault. But maybe it is. The end."

"Guys, how could tapping noises be Wally's fault?"

"We told Amelia our plan, but she did not say the right word to us, which is 'okay.' Or 'yes.' She thinks diversion will change our minds or get them off of the boxes, but she is wrong. This is why I am asking Molly Jane to get this bouncy ball rolling for us. The end and thank you. Molly Jane? Hello? Hello?!"

"Uh. . . ."

"THAT IS THE WRONG THING TO SAY! DO NOT SAY 'UH' AT US!"

"The right word to be saying now is 'okay,' Molly Jane, okay? Thank you!"

"I can't tell Amelia to move out of her house. I'm only ten."

"WRONG WORDS TO SAY! TEN HAS NOTHING TO DO WITH THIS THING!"

"Molly Jane, surely you can too say that thing to our Amelia! Go, Molly Jane, go!"

"UH OH! HERE IS ANOTHER HIT SINGLE! THEY JUST KEEP COMING!" Pip said.

Tap tap tap! I hear it and dread.
Tap-ping scares me out of my head!
Tap tap tap! It comes in the night.
Tap tap tap! It gives us a fright!
Tap tap, clickety fingers, I say.
The tapping is monsters, and we need to move away!

"*Also there is crunching,*" Teddy added. "*In the night called last, monsters started to do the crunching, too.*"

"CRUNCHY LIKE TOAST!" Pip hollered with his nose up against the camera again. Then he giggled. No matter what, Pip always giggles about toast.

"*Monsters have crunchy feet. Tee hee!*"

"CRUNCHY-CRUNCH-CRUNCH!"

"*Crunchy feet are funny! Feet are funny! Do you think feet are funny, Molly Jane? I do. And Pip does too! Even when we are scared out of our heads, we can tee hee about feet. Especially crunchy feet.*"

"You guys, hold on," I interrupted. "You aren't serious, are you? This is a joke. Right?"

"*SERIOUS IS WHAT WE ARE NOW! DO NOT THINK THAT WE ARE NOT! CLICKING MONSTERS WANT TO EAT US AND THAT IS NOT ONE BIT FUNNY!*"

"Monsters are not real. They are only made-up things, in books or movies."

"*Thank you for saying that thing, but Molly Jane,*" Teddy said quietly, "*we know that the tapping and clicking comes from monster fingers. We know. They are real as real can be.*"

"*DO NOT MAKE US MAD BY SAYING WE DON'T KNOW!*"

"I am almost totally sure that it is Benny Nubb who is tapping, definitely not monsters. I just need some more time to get proof. One more day. Just one. Can you guys give me one more day before you start talking about moving? It takes more than one day sometimes for a detective to —"

"DAY IS NOT THE TIME OF MONSTERS! MONSTERS DO THEIR BAD DEEDS AT NIGHT!" Pip squealed. "NIGHT AND NIGHT AND NIGHT, MOLLY JANE! TAP TAP TAP! TAP TAP TAP!"

"That's because he's in school during the day. It's Benny Nubb. I know it for almost sure. I just need to prove it, so —"

"We do not know about 'prove it,' or care much about that thing. But we surely know that the noises we hear are not made by the neighbor boy of Nubb, Molly Jane. They are instead made by scary floating monsters with clickety fingers and crunchy feet," Teddy interrupted. "Do not make us sad because you think we are lying. Do not say 'no' to us about the help we need, or else we will be sadder than sad."

"Teddy, no —"

"Molly Jane, yes!"

"I am not saying that you are lying. But I am ninety-nine percent sure it is him."

"I do not know what that means! Do not talk about numbers, please!"

"MOLLY JANE, DO NOT TALK TO US ABOUT THINGS CALLED PURR SENSE! THAT SOUNDS LIKE CAT STUFF, AND WE DO NOT LIKE IT! CAT-TALK HURTS OUR FEELINGS!"

"What I mean is, I am almost all the way sure. A percent is like. . . ." I scrunched up my brain. "It's a part of something."

"'PART OF' MEANS NOTHING TO GUINEA PIGS!"

"Molly Jane, what are you saying?"

"Think about a bucket of water —"

"Molly Jane, surely you know not to talk of buckets with Pip close by!"

"BUCKETS?! BUCKETS ARE WORST OF TIMES! MOM JANE PUTS US IN BUCKETS AND CALLS US . . . MONSTERS!!!!! WE ARE NOT MONSTERS! WE DO NOT HAVE CLICKY . . . FINGERS. . . . WELL, MAYBE WE DO HAVE THOSE THINGS, SOMETIMES. BUT WE ARE NOT MONSTERS!"

"Okay, okay! Calm down, guys. Never mind about buckets. Sorry. How about this? Think about a nice green salad."

"Good job, Molly Jane! We are calming right down with thoughts of salad. Yum!"

"SALAD IS BETTER! AND I WOULD LIKE SOME RIGHT NOW!"

"Take almost all of the salad and eat it all up. All that is left is one piece of lettuce that is brown on the edges and shrivelly. The good part, the part that you ate all up, is how sure I am that Benny Nubb is making the noises."

Teddy stared at me, scratched a bit, then waited as Pip appeared next to him, muttering about wanting a salad.

"So that means it is really close to for sure that the noises are not monsters at all, but are made by a mean boy who can only annoy you to pieces. That's what he does to me and other people all over my school."

Neigh-bor boy of Nubb
(Blub-blub-blub),

LEAVE. US. ALONE!
Neigh-bor boy of Nubb
(Blub-blub-blub),
LEAVE! US! ALONE!!!!

"Yes, Pip, that's right! Not monsters. Benny Nubb."

"THAT SONG OF NUBB IS MY NEWEST HIT SINGLE, MOLLY JANE! I WROTE IT JUST NOW. BUT WRITING THIS NUBB SONG DOES NOT MEAN THAT MY MIND IS CHANGED UP ABOUT MONSTERS! THE TAP-TAP-TAPS ARE MONSTER FINGERS, AND WE NEED TO PACK THE BOXES! LET'S GO!"

"The noises are made by Benny Nubb, and he can't hurt you."

"It is monsters. We know, Molly Jane. We know. Night and night and night. Our Wally made them very mad by cleaning them up and out of this house with his hammering and sawing. Now they are doing the revenge. We are pretty sure they have been hiding in Newark or Buffalo for some time. Now they are back. They do not like guinea pigs, Molly Jane. Or maybe they do — but it is the kind of liking like they want to eat us for a crunchy snack. We are in great danger and must pack up the brown boxes, like I keep saying to you. Tonight would be best. Soon. Before it gets darkly and those monsters come back to do their tapping. Okay, Molly Jane? You know our demands, so good luck. And thank you."

"DO NOT MAKE US MAD WITH QUESTIONS AND NOT BELIEVING, MOLLY JANE! DO NOT PUT YOURSELF ON THE THIN ICE! IT IS VERY COLD

AND WET THERE! DO NOT MAKE US THROW MAIL AT YOU!" As Pip finished yelling, Mom walked in to tell me that I needed to get ready to catch my bus.

"*Mom Jane! That is the voice of Mom Jane!*" Teddy squealed. "*We have so many, many worries in our little heads, and now there is Mom Jane, too!*" He backed up a bit, then said, "*Nice day, Mom Jane? The weather? It is good . . . for you?*"

"HELP, HELP, HELP, HELP! FIRST MONSTERS, NOW MOM JANE! WHAT NEXT? MOLLY JANE? WHY ARE YOU NOT SAVING THE DAY FOR US?! NO DAY IS GOOD WITH MOM JANE IN IT! MOM JANE PUTS EVERYONE IN BUCKETS!"

"Good morning, guinea pigs," Mom said, rolling her eyes. "It is a lovely day indeed. And Molly needs to get ready for school. Molly? Let's go."

"*Molly Jane? What about our demands? What about the boxes?!*"

"WORST OF TIMES! WORST OF TIMES!"

"Guys, I promise you, I am going to make the noises stop. Tonight." Whoops. Shouldn't have said that, either.

Chapter Five
Stuck between a casino and a home team

The Fourth Graders' State Fair will be held Friday, May 18 at 1:15-2:40 in the gym. All parents and other visitors are welcome to come at that time!

Projects will be graded on the following requirements:
I.   State Report — typed, double-spaced.
II. Political map — includes the capital and major cities.
III. Collage about your state — includes state symbols.
IV. Acrostic Poem
V.   Physical map — shows topography of your state, mountains, rivers, etc.
VI. A bar graph will be created in computer class. This graph will display the population of the ten largest cities in your state.

Projects will be judged (by 3rd and 5th grade students, as well as a panel of teachers) at the State Fair. The top three projects will receive awards: 2nd

place (red), 1st place (blue) and the Grand Prize ribbon (purple).
Good luck, students!

Ninety-nine kids from four fourth-grade classrooms were spread out around the edges of the gym having secret meetings. There are forty-nine state teams, plus one solo project. But don't feel sorry for the solo project person. It is a girl who wanted to do a solo project. Plus, she gets extra credit when it comes to the judging and grades. She is actually lucky not to have a partner to have to argue with. Almost all of the state teams I knew of were having arguments about their projects — including me and Nora, like I said before.

Anyway, we were having meetings while parent volunteers moved long tables into the middle for the fair. Everyone talked really quiet so no other team could overhear plans for the hardest part of the whole project: impressing kid judges. Yeah, we need to impress third and fifth graders. They all get a vote tomorrow about which state is the best.

Nora and I had been so busy getting the graded part of the project done perfectly that there had been no time to think about that part.

"I worked *so* hard on that map!" Nora had totally given up on new ideas. Instead, she decided to go on and on, once again, about the physical map (made out of salt dough) that had taken her and her mom fifteen trillion hours to finish. She made it sound like she had done more stuff for the project than me, which she hadn't. I had done the political map and the poem myself, plus a lot more work on the display, I think. Plus, we had agreed on who would do what in the beginning. "It took a whole day just to dry and now it is *perfect*," Nora bragged. "You'll see when you come over tonight, Molly. You'll love it."

My eyes wanted to roll really badly, but I stopped them in their tracks. Rolling eyes would make Nora mad at me and I did not need that. It was better to let her be braggy for now. I said, "Mmm hmm," instead.

"It isn't fair that Benji and Matt might win a ribbon just because they have show-off Nevada for a state."

"Why would they win?" I asked, looking out of the corner of my eye at those two, snickering and looking like they had the ribbon right in their bag, no problem.

"They're bringing a roulette wheel," Nora said. "A gambling machine. Matt's uncle works at a casino. It'll make the kid judges excited, and they'll forget about how cool the other projects are. Plus, they are plugging in flashy lights. I heard them talking in the lunch line today."

"No fair!" I said. I felt my insides get really tight at the thought of that unfairness.

"Mrs. Kelly said they could," Nora said glumly. "Molly, how are we supposed to get the grand prize ribbon with those show-offs next to us? What are we going to do?"

"I don't know," I mumbled. "Let me think."

"What if there are roulette wheels and flashing lights on both sides of us? Molly – we are between Nevada and New Jersey!"

"I know that," I said between my teeth. "I know the alphabetical order of this thing."

"We are in an impossible spot! Hannah and Kaylie are way luckier. They are in the far back and have the last state . . ."

I covered my face with my hands to block out the hopeless stuff Nora was tossing at me. "We'll think of something," I said through my fingers. "We will. We just have to. . . ." I thought for a while, then looked up and said, "We could add guinea pigs somehow. Guinea pigs always make people happy and —"

". . . the home state advantage, plus Las Vegas," Nora went on, not listening to me. "New Hampshire is not going to win against all of that. Not even if we put the cutest guinea pigs ever in the project."

"Why are you being so darned negative?" I snapped, which made Nora clamp her mouth shut really tight and cross her arms at me. I softened up my voice. "Let's think of something good instead of only talking about how impossible it is going to be to win. Okay? There has to be something better than flashy lights and a roulette wheel."

"If you spent more time thinking about winning and not so much about Benny Nubb," Nora said, which made all the hairs on my neck and arms stick up, "then maybe we would not be stuck with a not-exciting project in an impossible place, sure to lose tomorrow!"

My eyes popped open wide. "I cannot believe you said that, Nora Sutter! I've only spent one half day on the case so far, and how can it be my fault that New Hampshire is between those two states in the alphabet? That is ridiculous!"

"That's not what I meant, Molly. Good grief. Don't be dumb."

Oh my gosh, did she just call me dumb?

I was so tired of this project driving me and my best friend apart. I took some deep breaths and tried my hardest not to be mad at Nora.

Think, Molly, think. Think of something.

I couldn't think of anything in that buzzing gym with her sitting there, mad at me again. I added that new problem to my list of things to think about later today. My list was already long, and my head was about to explode on me. I really needed to write stuff in my notebook to clear some space in my head. I pretended to do that, writing in my imagination.

Teddy and Pip are afraid of monsters now. They want me to tell Amelia to move out of the house. Amelia has a book deadline, and I have a State Fair deadline. We are in the same rocky boat, trying to keep life preservers on the guinea pigs.

Benny Nubb did not seem tired today. Why not? He would have to be really tired after doing stuff into the early hours of the morning, wouldn't he? He was still a human, even if he was a mean one, and humans need sleep. But he was doing his usual mean stuff, like, every time I saw him. I didn't notice him yawning a lot, or anything like that.

He had accomplices. Who? What if every boy in the fifth grade was helping him?! If that was true, there would be evidence.

I sat up a little straighter after that thought.

If all kinds of boys were tapping on Amelia's windows, they would mess up the plants and stuff and leave footprints! Lots of boys could not possibly be neat enough to not leave any clues behind. I need to check on that.

My eyes shifted to Nora's, which were little squinty slits at me. Somehow she knew I was thinking about the case. Best friends can read minds like that.

And then, there *he* was, peeking in the gym with a bunch of friends around him. "Hey, Molly Fisher!" he called.

I looked away really fast, my face scrunched into a big hot frown.

"What state do you have? The state of confusion?" Benny and his friends thought that joke was funny. It wasn't. It was really dumb.

Nora rolled her eyes. But not with me, because we were not even going to share feelings about Benny Nubb today. Even though it was hardly my fault that he decided to tease me in front of a zillion people. Nora was being unreasonable and impossible and thought it was my fault anyway.

I looked at the middle of the gym and counted seventeen long tables set up in neat rows. Each table was divided into three spots for three different states. The state name was being taped to the front of the table on a piece of red, white, or blue paper. In the front were tables for Alabama, Alaska and Arizona, and across from them were Arkansas, California and Colorado. Alphabetical order would put New Hampshire right smack in the middle. In the middle, between two show-off states.

Darn it.

How unlucky could we get? Nora was right, it was a terrible spot!

I tried to think of a way to make our project more interesting to the kids than the others were, but my brain would not cooperate. Rats.

It *is* a good state with good qualities — it really is! It is pretty, has lots of nature going on, and they have lots of granite there. Mom says people (grown-ups) love granite. And the first presidential primary. . . .

Maybe guinea pigs holding flags would be a good idea. Guinea pigs showing different state symbols? Maybe, after I solved the mystery, Teddy and Pip could help me with some pictures. . . .

"I have the orthodontist today." Nora decided to talk to me again. "I won't be on the bus. Come over after you're home and we can work on some crafts. I have some ideas for headbands. At least that is something. At least I am trying."

I didn't argue with her about who was and was not trying. What was the point of that? "Okay."

"If you care about this project and winning the ribbon, you'll come *right* over," Nora said and her eyes were laser beams on me. "We have a lot of work to do tonight, and Mom won't let me stay up late."

I almost said "yes ma'am." That's how bossy she sounded.

Good grief.

Chapter Six
Monsters do not care about deadlines

Amelia's fingers hovered over the keys with the unfinished chapter in front of her. The main character's thoughts had stopped mid-sentence as the kitchen clock tick-tick-ticked on and her deadline grew nearer and nearer.

"*Amelia? Are you hearing me? Your bad guy needs to go to the jail. That is where bad guys need to be. Put him in there, okay? Do that for Teddy. And thank you!*"

"*AMELIA? WHY ARE YOU NOT TYPING? TYPE TYPE TYPE, AMELIA! MAKE THE BAD GUY GET HIS EARS PECKED BY A CLAW-FOOTED BIRD!*" Pip suggested. "*PECK PECK PECK! PECK PECK PECK! TEE HEE! WHY ARE YOU NOT TYPING THAT THING I SAID?*"

"Darlings, isn't it time for your favorite cartoon program?" Amelia asked desperately.

"*Nope.*"

"*NO, AMELIA! WE ARE FINE HERE!*"

"Or perhaps you would like a little treat?"

"*Thank you! A treat would be nice,*" Teddy said. "*But also I am thinking that you are trying to get rid of your best friends called Teddy and Pip, and that might hurt my feelings somewhat. And Pip's, too, maybe."

"VEGGIES, VEGGIES, VEGGIES!" Pip squealed. "BUT WE ARE NOT GOING ANYWHERE! NICE TRY!"

"Oh, no, darlings, no." Amelia stroked Teddy's little nose. "I am not trying to do that. Not at all. It's just that I have a deadline, and I'm finding it difficult to . . . to think . . . very well."

"We will help you with the thinking. It is no problem. What do you need us to think about, Amelia?"

"TELL US NOW! WE DO NOT HAVE ALL DAY!"

Amelia's mouth opened, then closed again. She shook her head. "I appreciate your offers, darlings, but the words in my story really must be my own, since my name will be on the cover —"

"That is no problem, Amelia. You can put our names, too, on the cover. That's okay."

"PIP IS A ROCK STAR, AND NOW A BOOK-WRITER, TOO! BEST OF TIMES!"

"Boys, I really must finish this chapter by this evening. And it would help me immensely if you two would please give me some time alone."

"But Amelia, we are going to be the thing called 'together,' not alone. You said —"

"Yes, but I would only be in the next room, so you would not really be alone at all."

"There are monsters out there," Teddy whispered. "Monsters will stay away only if you are with us. And it is safest in this kitchen because monsters do not like kitchens. For some reason. Or other. So we are staying with our Amelia. In the kitchen."

"Darlings, I have a deadline —"

"MONSTERS DO NOT CARE ABOUT DEADLINES! THOSE THINGS ONLY MAKE THEM MADDER AND MADDEST!"

"Alright, alright. We will stay in the kitchen, together," Amelia sighed. "I will set out a snack right here."

"THANK YOU, BEST FRIEND AMELIA!"

"I love you, Amelia!"

"I thought that we had decided that the monsters, if they existed — which they don't — only bother us at night," Amelia said quietly, trying not to sound weary.

"The monsters do their tapping only at night," Teddy explained. "But always they are around — always! They turn the thing called 'invisible' and peek in windows all the day long. They do! Surely they do!"

"MONSTERS ARE WATCHING! THEY HAVE MANY EYES! MANY!!"

"We are happy that the one smallish window here in this kitchen is now covered up with those chicken-decorated towels. Thank you for that! Monsters cannot see us in here. Plus, I believe they are afraid of chickens."

"CHICKENS ARE SCARY!"

Amelia pushed back her chair and went to the refrigerator. As she chose vegetables and set them on the counter, the guinea pigs continued to chatter away about this and that, about chickens and monsters.

Oh, how she wished that Wally were here.

Two more days. . . .

Their talks in the evening, times when Teddy and Pip crowded against the phone to hear his voice, were so soothing. Oh, she missed him so.

TAP TAP TAP . . . TAP TAP TAP!

Amelia dropped the bag of vegetables as the guinea pigs began to whoop and wheek.

TAP TAP TAP . . . TAP TAP TAP!

"MONSTERS! IN THE DAY! IN THE LIGHT! AMELIA!"

"*Daytime tapping, Amelia! We need to pack the boxes! Now or sooner!*"

"Boys, that was not . . . not the same thing. It wasn't. It was . . . um . . ."

"*Amelia, it was too!*"

"*IT WAS THE SAME!*"

The taps seemed to have stopped again. Amelia closed her eyes and rubbed her forehead. If only she could have some time to herself today. But how?

"*Hi, Amelia!*" Teddy said.

"NICE DAY, AMELIA? THE VEGGIES? THEY ARE COMING ALONG NICELY? TODAY?"

"*Amelia? Amelia? Amelia?*"

"EXCUSE ME, AMELIA! WE ARE WAITING FOR THAT SNACK! THANK YOU!"

"Oh, of course! Goodness," she murmured, then finished rinsing and drying the vegetables. She set them on the walkway next to Teddy and Pip.

How could she get some time alone?

Chapter Seven
Nothing but trouble

"Benny Nubb told me to tell you to stop looking at him, because he doesn't want a girlfriend." Hannah said this in a giggly whisper, right in my ear.

"What?" I jerked away fast and my mouth fell open really wide. I was shocked all the way down to my shoes to hear something like that. "What?!" I said again.

"Whatever you do, don't turn around right now!" Hannah went on, trying really hard to get her giggles under control. "He's looking right at you, Molly!"

I made a face, rubbed at my forehead, then said, "You have got to be kidding me."

"Nope. Sorry, Molly, but I am not kidding. He noticed you watching him and got the wrongest possible idea."

"'Wrongest' isn't a word," I said, and she giggled, of course. "Oh my gosh," I groaned. "How am I supposed to finish the case if he's noticing that I'm watching him?"

Hannah did a shrug that hardly had any sympathy in it.

"I need your help."

"Me?"

"Yes, you. I really, really need to set up a video recording tonight, to do more surveillance. It's the only way to catch him in the act. Can you do that for me?"

"Me?" Hannah squeaked again. "Why me?"

"Because your bedroom window is the perfect place for it."

"Yeah, well —"

"And I have to be at Nora's tonight, as soon as possible, to finish up the project. If she finds out I am working on the case. . . . I have no idea how much more mad she can get, and I do not want to find out."

"I don't know, Molly," Hannah said. "I have a project to finish too. I am going to Kaylie's to work on Wyoming tonight. You and Nora aren't the only ones who want a ribbon, you know."

"But the difference is that Kaylie isn't totally mad at you. And Benny Nubb isn't thinking totally backwards things about why you're watching him."

"You know, Nora has been in a bad mood lately, like the last two days. Especially today."

"Having her braces tightened up won't make her in a better one, either." We both sighed then I changed the subject. "What are you guys doing to impress judges?" I asked. Hannah got real quiet after I asked that question and I remembered that friends were keeping secrets all over the place now. "Never mind. I'll find out tomorrow. I'll tell you what we're doing: nothing. We don't have a single good idea. Except making headbands, I guess."

"Headbands?"

I shrugged.

"Look, Molly, I'll try to set up the video recording for you," Hannah said, finally finding some sympathy in her heart. "But don't get your hopes up very high. I'd have to use Jordan's camera and he's really suspicious of me after last night. Honestly, I think we have to wait until the weekend to do this stuff. Tonight is a bad night for solving a case, don't you think? Tomorrow's the State Fair."

"I totally, totally know that, Hannah! But it has to be tonight. I promised. Things are really bad for my friends, and I don't know if Amelia can stand it for one more night."

"Yeah, well, good luck, Molly. For real. Hey, are you free on Saturday? Mom said I could have a sleepover."

"My mom is probably inviting Max and his . . . his girlfriend over." I wrinkled up my nose.

"Oh. Wait a minute, did you say your cousin Max has a *girlfriend*?" Hannah giggled.

"Not really." I shrugged.

"Not really?"

"No. He doesn't. It isn't . . . like that. No way."

"Well? What is it like? What's she like?"

I stopped myself from saying she probably giggled a lot and wore pink clothes, because that is how Hannah is herself, about eighty-six percent of the time. "I'm sure she only cares about make-up and clothes and that kind of stuff. I don't know why Max would like somebody like that." Hannah didn't have anything to say back so I switched back to the case. "I have to solve this mystery, and it has to be tonight, Hannah. I have never given up on something before, and I don't want to start now. I have to find a way to do it all. I just have to."

She gave me another sympathetic look that really didn't help.

"Hey, Molly Fisher!"

Oh my gosh. Oh, darn it. That was Benny Nubb, yelling at me from the back of the bus.

"If you want my autograph, all you gotta do is ask!"

I rolled my eyes and looked out the window.

"Poor Molly," Hannah said.

"Well? Do you?" he shouted, then laughed with all of his friends.

I was so embarrassed and mad I felt like I had a temperature of a million degrees. When the bus stopped, I hurried off after Hannah, making sure not to look behind me or get my eyeballs anywhere near to Benny Nubb.

I was only going to quickly look around the front of Amelia's house for clues, then rush home, get my stuff and go to Nora's. But I didn't even get a start before I heard his loud voice again.

"Hey! Molly Fisher! Whatcha doin'?"

Oh, darn it! Why was he watching every step I took today? The plan was ruined. A detective can't look for clues about a suspect right under his eyeballs. If I didn't go inside Amelia's house now, he would be more suspicious than ever, so even though I hadn't planned on it, now I had to. Don't get me wrong — I love going to Amelia and Wally's cute little house, and I love seeing Teddy and Pip. But this afternoon, I didn't have time. Plain and simple. I had a billion things on my back and on my mind, and Nora was going to be so mad at me.

"Molly Fisher! Hey!"

Ugh. I gritted my teeth, real tight, did not turn around, then rushed to the steps and knocked on the door.

Amelia had her phone against her chest. She looked super tired, but smiled at me nicely anyway. "One moment," she said to her caller, then said, "Molly, how lovely of you to stop by!"

"Hi, Amelia," I said, feeling squirmy guilt because I hadn't meant to stop by at all.

"Come on in, Molly. I need to finish this call, then I'll be right with you." She smiled again. "The boys are . . . uh. . . . Well, they're hiding under an igloo near the refrigerator. I'm sure they'll be thrilled to see you."

I let my backpack slide off of my back and onto the floor. Hiding (when they weren't playing hide-and-seek) was a bad sign. It was a sign of being scared.

Wally and Amelia's house is the cutest and coolest ever. Wally fixed it up, so it went from being the neighborhood's empty haunted house to being the coziest, guinea-pig-friendliest house ever. What do I mean by that? Well, for one thing, he built a walkway all around the downstairs for the guinea pigs. That means they can walk from room to room whenever they want to. They can safely peek over the ledge, which is see-through, so they never have to miss a thing.

Hiding in the kitchen under an igloo, with all of that other cool and fun space to use, meant that the guys were more scared than ever.

I stepped into the usually sunny and cheerful kitchen. Today, with the sun behind clouds, it was dark and gloomy. Amelia had closed up the red and white checkered curtains and also covered the window with towels. The towels had chickens on them.

Quiet whispers came from the purple plastic igloo.

"Guys? It's Molly." I whispered too.

I saw two noses, then heard, "*Hi, Molly Jane.*"

"*WHERE IS AMELIA?*"

"*Yes, Molly Jane, what has happened to our Amelia? Why is she not here in this safe kitchen?*"

"She's in the living room, talking on the phone," I said, trying not to frown too much about this not-very-welcoming welcome.

"*PHONES ARE NO GOOD! ALWAYS SHE IS TALKING ON THAT THING! WORST OF TIMES!*"

"*Are you surely sure, Molly Jane, that that is what is going on? Amelia is talking on that phoney-phone, and . . . and . . . please tell us that monsters did not get her. Please!*"

"Teddy, of course monsters didn't get her. There are no such things are monsters. She's right there, in the living room. If you listen you can hear her talking. Okay? Now let's hang out."

Teddy and Pip inched their way out of the igloo, then very slowly crept along the walkway toward the living room. When they saw and heard Amelia and knew she was okay, they dashed back to the igloo.

"*Living room is not a safe place, Molly Jane! This kitchen is the one and only safe place in this haunted house! Tell Amelia! Tell her!*"

"Amelia is fine," I said. "And you guys are especially safe when there are towels over the window, so you did a good job with that."

Two little heads turned to look at the towels. "*KITCHEN IS SAFE BECAUSE THERE ARE PECKING CHICKENS ON THOSE TOWELS,*" Pip said in a noisy whisper. "*I SAID THIS THING TO AMELIA. MONSTERS ARE AFRAID OF THOSE THINGS. PIP IS SOME AFRAID OF THEM TOO.*"

"*Well? What is this 'hang out' that you want to do, Molly Jane?*" Teddy whispered.

"How about we talk?"

"*WHAT DO YOU WANT TO TALK ABOUT, MOLLY JANE? HURRY UP! WE DO NOT HAVE ALL DAY, YOU KNOW! MONSTERS ARE COMING, AND WE ARE VERY BUSY WITH OUR MOVING PLANS!*"

My feelings were really feeling stepped on now. "I need someone to talk to about my bad day. I thought maybe you guys would care, or at least listen. Or maybe have a diversion out of it."

"*Your day, Molly Jane, was not good?*"

"Worse than not good. I have so much stress that I think I am going to go cuckoo," I said.

"*ALRIGHT, THEN. TELL US YOUR PROBLEMS, MOLLY JANE! WE DO NOT NEED FOR YOU TO GO THE THING OF CUCKOO ON US. WE HAVE OTHER PROBLEMS TOO, YOU KNOW!*"

I pulled a chair up to the walkway. "Well, the biggest problem is my school project about New Hampshire."

"What are you saying, Molly Jane? What is this thing?"

"NO GOOD!"

"It's homework. I have been working on it forever, and it has to be ready for tomorrow. We are having a State Fair at school."

"NO FAIR!"

"This fair, it is a time of games and fun? Food and clowns?"

"CLOWNS ARE SCARY, MOLLY JANE! DO NOT DO THE FAIR!"

"It isn't that kind of a fair. It's at school, in the gym, and teams give presentations about their states, and judges give ribbons to the best ones. My state is New Hampshire."

"MOLLY JANE SHOULD GET EVERY RIBBON!"

"Thanks, Pip."

"WHAT IS A RIBBON ABOUT?"

"It's about being the best. It's a prize."

"OKAY, THEN! THE END! WHAT ELSE IS WRONG?"

"There are forty-nine other states that want to win too."

"*Forty-nine sounds like many,*" Teddy said. "*Too many. I am not liking that there are so many of those states.*"

"WORST OF TIMES!"

"Anyway, Nora and I are partners, and so that is wrecking our friendship. We really want to win a ribbon. It is making us stressed out at each other. We need to have more oomph to impress the judges, but we don't have a single good idea. The states on both sides of us are show-offs and will have flashy stuff. New Hampshire is great, but there isn't anything flashy that we know about it."

Teddy scratched his ear with a back foot. "Molly Jane, what means 'oomph'?" he asked.

"OOMPH!" Pip giggled. "OOMPH! I WILL WRITE A SONG ABOUT OOMPH!"

"Oomph means . . . exciting. Like, it gives you the feeling you get about veggies."

"WE LIKE VEGGIES!"

"Yes, I know how that feelings feels," Teddy agreed. "Best of times. Your thing should be all about veggies if you want a ribbon. Your troubles are fixed now. You're welcome."

"THERE ARE BOXES TO PACK, MOLLY JANE! REMEMBER OUR DEMANDS FROM EARLY IN THIS DAY?"

"Pip —"

"MOLLY JANE! BOXES!"

"So sorry about Pip's no manners. We care very much about the sad times you are having with your school stuff and your need for 'oomph.' We, too, are having hard and sad times, so we know how these things go. When you are done telling of your troubles with the Ham Shires, we will tell you more about the monsters who are trying to eat us all up."

"CRUNCHY-CRUNCH-CRUNCH, MOLLY JANE! CRUNCHY-CRUNCH-CRUNCH!"

"Guys, the noises are made by your neighbor, Benny Nubb, like I told you this morning."

"If the tapping is done by that Nubb you speak of, they will be done this night, right Molly Jane? Is that what you are saying to us? Is that a promise?

Because you said to us some time ago in this day that the mystery would be solved and done. You said that thing. But if the noises are not done, then they are monster fingers and we will be crunched up. Right?"

My stomach felt tight as I remembered that promise. If I didn't solve the mystery, catch Benny Nubb in the act, and have proof to show these guys, they would be more sure than ever that monsters were tapping on their windows. The pressure was squeezing on me now. Plus, Nora was waiting for me down the street, getting even madder at me, probably. What was I supposed to do? I wished someone could tell me.

"Right?" Teddy said again.

"Um. . . ."

"*YOU DID NOT SAY THE WORD OF 'RIGHT'! MOLLY JANE, WHAT ARE YOU SAYING TO US INSTEAD?!*"

Amelia popped into the room just then, so I was saved from answering. She looked happy and was smiling kind of a lot, actually. It made me feel some hope for the first time all day. "Sorry about that call, everyone. It was my editor. Oh my goodness, she is frantic because I am so behind! But never mind that. I have good news," she said.

"*GOOD IS MY FAVORITE KIND OF NEWS!*" Pip squealed.

"*What is the news, Amelia?! What? What? What?!*"

Amelia smoothed her hair and did a little laugh at the guinea pigs' excitement. "I didn't get a chance to tell you this before that long phone call, but I spoke with Max earlier, and he has agreed to come by tonight."

I waited for Teddy and Pip to start squealing and complaining about that. Why would Amelia think this was good news? Was everyone going cuckoo today?

But, after a bit more silence, Pip started to sing. Yes, sing. "*MAX IS A DUDE WHO EATS. . . .*" He turned his little head in my direction, then said, "*NO! NO! NO! I MEAN, MAX IS NO GOOD! BOO! BAD IDEA! TELL US SOME DIFFERENT NEWS, AMELIA!*"

"*Amelia, we need for you to stay with us! We need 'together,' or else we need to go to Molly Jane's safe house instead of here. Max coming here will not help matters. Max and also tapping, clicking monsters is not good news.*"

"Boys, please listen. I am desperately in need of some time to finish my chapter. I appreciate the help you gave me this afternoon, but there is more to do, and you need to understand that writing a book is something a person must do, at least in part, alone."

"*ALONE IS NO GOOD,*" Pip said softly.

"I know Max isn't your first choice of a companion," Amelia continued, "but Molly here is so terribly busy, and Max is free tonight."

"I could come . . ." I started, but had to stop myself in my tracks. I couldn't come over tonight — no way! No more promises.

Amelia ducked down to look her guinea pigs in the eyes. "Would it sweeten up the idea if I included Sophie? Or, rather, if Max included Sophie?" Amelia's smile reminded me of Mom's from this morning, when she was giggling about Max and that girl with Aunt Patty.

"*We love the Sophie, Amelia! She is sweet!*"

"THE SOPHIE IS PRETTY AND SMART AND THE DEAL IS SWEET, AMELIA!" Pip squeaked. "*OH! OH! I KNOW! THE SOPHIE WILL KNOW HOW TO KEEP THOSE MONSTERS AWAY! THE SOPHIE WILL SAVE THE DAY! YES, IT IS A GOOD IDEA AND GOOD NEWS, AMELIA! LISTEN, HERE COMES ANOTHER HIT SINGLE!*" And Pip started to sing.

> *Sophie will come,*
> *Monsters will go.*
> *Don't ask how,*
> *'Cuz I just know!*

Huh? Whoa. I felt like a balloon with all the air leaking out. I could not believe this. I had just been fired or replaced by some giggling, girly-girl stranger named Sophie. Teddy and Pip *loved* her and thought she was the one to solve the mystery? Huh? And they didn't even seem to mind that they had to spend time with Max, too. That's how much they loved her. I am not the type to cry if I can help it, but my throat was super tight just then. Plus my eyes were prickly. Those are the first signs of crying about to start. "I need to get home," I said, and I sounded like a girl who was about to cry. Darn it.

"Molly, I realize that I asked you to look into the whole situation, but it was unfair of me to ask during such a busy time. You go ahead and work on your project tonight, and don't worry about us. I am sure it will be a huge success and can't wait to see it. I promise to stop by the fair tomorrow afternoon." Amelia smiled. She didn't even notice my almost-crying. When her phone rang, the guinea pigs ducked into the purple igloo and she left the room.

"*Bye, Molly Jane!*"

"*DO NOT LET MONSTERS SNEAK IN WHEN YOU GO OUT!*" Pip squealed.

Chapter Eight
Murphy's law

They loved Sophie, huh? Well, fine. I was still the detective around here, not her. And I was more determined than ever to solve the mystery. So, even though I knew Nora would be upset because I was not at her house yet, I went back to clue-finding in front of Amelia's house.

There wasn't much to see, and it was hard to do detective work with my backpack brushing against stuff. I looked and looked, but the more I looked, the more I knew that there was nothing to find. There were no signs of fifth-grade boy mischief, like finger or nose prints on the window, candy or gum wrappers, shoe prints, wrecked plants, or anything. There was nothing to see but okay-looking plants (as far as I knew; I am not a plant doctor) with rocks under them, and Amelia's two bird feeders. In the window was a red bird decoration of some kind. No sign of mischief of any kind caught my eyes.

Oh my gosh, there was that mean boy again! Why wouldn't he leave me alone for two seconds? He watched me from his bike in his driveway.

"Hey, Molly Fisher!" he yelled. "I'll vote for you tomorrow if you give me ten dollars!"

I scrunched up my face then turned my back on him. What he just suggested was called "bribing a judge," and his stupid vote only counted for a little tiny bit anyway. It would never be worth it in a zillion years to cheat like that for ten dollars. How dumb did he think I was?

That was not a question I actually wanted an answer to. I had to put that Benny Nubb out of my head. I had no time for him now, had to make my brain focus only on New Hampshire and the purple ribbon. What could we do to give our project some oomph? What about guinea pigs? Nora had not given my idea a second of her time, but it was a good one. Guinea pigs made people stop and look, and always smile. But how exactly could I . . . ?

I had been thinking so hard that I was surprised to find myself in my own driveway. Daddy calls that "autopilot." I stopped in my tracks when I saw Max's shiny red car there.

I went in the back door. "Mom? I'm home," I called. "I stopped at Amelia's first. That's why —"

"Just a minute, Molly!" Mom called from upstairs. Then I heard a girl's voice coming from my living room. A giggly, happy girl's voice. That plus Max's car in the driveway equaled this: Sophie was here, in my house, right now.

"*Hello! Pretty, pretty, pretty! Pretty bird! BIRDIE! BIRDIE!*"

"Hi, Tweets," I said glumly, dropping my backpack on the floor by the table. "What is going on around here?"

Tweets started to peck at the door of his cage like he does. He wanted to get out. "*Pretty? Birdie? Birdie, birdie?*"

Mom bustled into the kitchen, smelling like perfume and dressed up like she was on her way to a party. Which made no sense at all. She hung a black clothing bag over the door.

I crossed my arms. "What's going on? What's that for?" I pointed at the black bag.

Mom checked her fancy jeweled watch, then ducked down to put her hands on my shoulders. She looked into my eyes with totally sorry ones of her own. That was not a good sign. "Daddy and I need to go downtown for an important dinner tonight with some work people from out of town."

"You . . . what?" My eyes felt humongous. "Downtown? Tonight?"

"I know!" she said, shaking her head then sneaking a look up at the kitchen clock. "It is so last-minute, and such bad timing!"

"Mom!"

"Daddy's boss and his wife were supposed to entertain these clients tonight, but Mr. Parker had something or other come up. But that's life, sometimes," she said, nodding, waiting for me to agree. "We have to roll with it, sometimes."

I frowned.

"Molly?"

"You were going to help me with my project tonight, and also make cards for Nanna and all the other grandmas!"

"I know, honey," Mom sighed. "And I'm sorry. But I am sure that Mrs. Sutter can help you girls tonight."

"But...."

"And the Grandma Club can go one visit with no cards. They love to see you so much, Molly. Your presence is enough of a present." She smiled about that pun, but I didn't. "Anyway, I need to leave really soon or I will be stuck in traffic here *and* there. I'm meeting Daddy at his office so he can change. You're disappointed," she said.

"Um, yeah."

"I am so sorry, Molly. I wish I could be in both places at once."

"*Hello? Hello! Pretty? Birdie?*"

"That girl isn't staying here, is she?" I made my voice as quiet as I could get it. "Only Max is going to stay with me, right? Like usual?"

Mom's expression did not say "yes."

"Amelia told me that Max and that girl are going to her house tonight, to be with Teddy and Pip while she goes to the library," I said.

"Well, those plans have changed," Mom said, distracted, eyeballs moving from the clock to the clothes bag. "Oh my gosh, I forgot Daddy's shoes!"

"Why don't you tell Max that *she* can go to Amelia's and he can stay here with me?" I suggested.

"Honey, the two of them gave up their own evening plans to help us. Which is very kind." She stopped and looked at me a long time until guilty squirmy feelings started up. "I think we need to work on being grateful. Now, I need to run upstairs and get those shoes, then get going."

I frowned some more and looked away from her. It had seemed like a perfect idea, for that girl to go to Amelia's. Teddy and Pip apparently loved her to pieces and thought she could solve all of their problems in two seconds, so why not let them have her tonight? And I could have Max because he was . . . he was . . . he was *mine*. He had always been mine. It was no fair that. . . . My eyes felt stingy and hot again. Darn it.

"*Pretty, pretty, pretty!*"

"Tweets, just hang on. Wait until Mom goes," I said through teeth that were probably tighter than Nora's. Nora! Oh, darn it! I needed to get to her house. How many problems was a person supposed to handle all in one swoop, anyway?

There was more giggling coming from the living room, then Mom's voice and fast high-heeled shoes clicking. "Thank you *so much*, Max and Sophie!" Mom called. "I'll call to check in once I meet up with Dan. Molly's in the kitchen." She reappeared by me with two big black shoes, one in each hand, and gave me a hug with those shoes bumping into my back a little bit. "Did you know that Sophie is studying to be a teacher?"

I mumbled something about that and hugged her back. "Please don't go," I said in the whispery-est whisper.

But Mom didn't hear me. "Get to bed early, okay? Tomorrow is a big day."

No kidding. It was the biggest day I had had in a long time.

Mom's cell phone rang and she answered the call while finishing the weird shoe-hug. "I love you, honey," she said, kissing my cheek. "Be good." Then she grabbed the black bag, shoved the shoes into it, and said, "I know, Dan, I know. I'm on my way!"

"*Pretty, pretty!*" Tweets reminded me, so I opened his door, and he flew on top of my head. "*Hello! Hello, pretty!*"

"Hi, Tweets," I said, holding a finger up and waiting for him to hop on. He stayed on my head.

"*Pretty bird! Pretty, pretty, pretty! Pretty birdie! Birdie, birdie!*"

"I know you're pretty. Please get off my head." I held up a finger again. Now I had one more person to disappoint because I had no time for playing. I had to get him back in the cage in about fifteen seconds. "I'll hang out with you for a little bit, but I need to get to Nora's before...."

I could not believe it. Tweets ignored my finger, flew off of my head, and right into the living room.

"Oh! Look, it's Paulie!" that girl said. "Hi, Paulie! Hi, sweetie!"

Why in the world was she calling my *boy* bird Polly?

"Molly? Mol? Where are you?" Max did not sound like his normal self. He sounded too loud and too happy to be himself. "Your bird's out here! Where are you? Come on out! I want you to meet Sophie!"

Well, what about what I wanted? Did anyone care about that tonight? I did not want to meet Sophie. I was almost one hundred percent full of stress, and it was all I could do to have the teeniest bit of manners. Maybe I did not even have that much. I wanted to skip this part so, so, so much. But running upstairs to my room or out the door to Nora's right now would probably be a bad idea and cause more problems, wouldn't it? Yeah, for sure. That's how it is when you're ten. I had to get it over with. I had to meet her and tell Max the plan, and *then* I could leave.

My eyes got wide as I spotted Max. Why? Because unless he is eating at our kitchen table or digging in the fridge, Max is always flopped on the couch in front of the TV in his comfortable clothes. Today, he was not only standing up, but also pacing back and forth. He was not wearing the usual comfortable clothes, either. He was wearing a white shirt. All white. The kind with buttons. It was blinding my eyeballs, it was so white. Plus it was ironed. His jeans looked new and not comfortable. To finish it all up, he had brown shoes on his feet – the loafer kind that Daddy wears to work. My cool cousin Max looked like an office worker at Daddy's company. Besides all that, he had a haircut. And . . . was he wearing cologne? Yuck!

The girl, Sophie, wasn't as girly-looking as I had imagined (there was no pink stuff on her, and she didn't have a bunch of jewelry or make-up). She had medium-length hair and was wearing jeans and a blue shirt. She looked pretty normal, actually. She was looking at our family pictures on the fireplace shelf, her eyes on the one of Nanna and Grandpa Joe. Tweets was on her shoulder (not on her head), talking quietly about how pretty he was (instead of screaming about it, for a change).

"He couldn't talk on Sunday, but now he can!" she commented. "That is so amazing! Paulie, you pretty bird, you are amazing!"

"*Pretty, pretty, pretty!*" Tweets started bobbing his head up and down real fast, like he does when he is totally excited. And like when he totally loves someone.

"I need to go to Nora's house," I said, my voice sounding super tight.

"Here she is! Here's Molly!" Max ignored what I had said about going to Nora's. He clapped his hands and smiled real big, then held his hand out like he was saying "welcome to the show!" He was acting like a totally goofy game show host. "Sophie, this is Molly, my cousin. And Mol, this is Sophie, my . . . uh . . . my . . . uh. . . ."

"Hi," I interrupted, because apparently this new dressed-up Max couldn't finish that really tough sentence.

"Hi, Molly!" Sophie's big smile got even bigger. She set the picture back in its place. "It is so nice to meet you! I've heard so much about you!" She looked at Max then back at me.

I wondered what in the world Max had been saying to her about me. "Hmm," I mumbled instead of saying something nicer. I knew I needed to be more polite, because Max had probably made me sound like a really cool person, but I couldn't do it. It was like the nice and polite part of me had been switched off, and the stressed-up part had taken over. "Max? I need to go to Nora's," I repeated.

Max said, "Yeah, your mom told me about that. But I thought we could maybe hang out first. We could get a pizza and get to know each other. Just the three of us."

"Four of us!" Sophie chimed in, now holding a Tweets with good manners on her finger.

"*Hello!*" Tweets said, and Sophie giggled.

"Right. The three of us plus Mr. Feathers," said the game show host.

"Nora needs me to come over. Now," I said, not looking at Sophie. "Not after dinner. You have no idea how mad she can get if I don't. . . ." I stopped and tried to calm myself down for a few seconds. "Plus, I don't know how long I'll be over there. We have a huge pile of stuff to do. So go ahead and have pizza without me." I tried to look at Sophie and give her a smile, but my mouth felt too tight to curve up.

"But Mol, I mean, you gotta eat," Max said, sounding nervous, probably because Mom had told him he had to make sure of it.

"I'll eat over there. Or . . . well, I know how to make a sandwich," I mumbled. "See ya later." I headed to the kitchen to get my backpack.

Max followed me, because the phone was ringing in the there. He answered the call really fast then stopped me from leaving by grabbing my backpack so I couldn't keep walking. "Hang on, Mol, it's for you," he said. "It's a . . . Mrs. Sutter?"

Why was Nora's mom calling me? I found out two seconds after I put the phone to my ear. "Nora's sick, sweetheart."

I sank onto a chair. Sick? *Sick?* Of all the things Nora could be. . . . The word didn't make any sense. Nora couldn't be. Why would she be? She had been okay this afternoon, arguing with me in the gym.

"What kind?" I asked, my voice a whisper.

"She got back from the orthodontist and threw up."

"The orthodontist made her throw up?"

"Oh, no, honey. Her brother has been sick, and I guess she caught it. Probably a twenty-four hour virus."

"Twenty-four hours? Oh no," I groaned, doing fast math. "Oh. No."

"I know, Molly. The State Fair is tomorrow." Mrs. Sutter sounded sorry now. "You girls worked so hard. Well, it is what it is. I called Mrs. Kelly, so she knows, and . . ."

"But —"

". . . have to wait twenty-four hours after the fever goes down. I'm sorry, sweetie, but I need to get back to my sick kids. Oh, she told me that you need to pick up some things for tomorrow. I'll leave it all on the front step, if that's alright. Probably best if you don't come inside with all the germs flying around in here." Click.

"But. . . ." I kept the phone by my ear, hoping to hear something else, something better, but all I heard was that dial tone. "Mrs. Sutter?"

Max said, "Mol? What happened now?"

I did not answer him. There was a crack of thunder as I slowly put the phone back in its holder. Nora was sick. She was not going to be at the fair tomorrow. I had worked so hard for so, so, so long on that darned project and now I had ten bazillion things to do with no help. And tomorrow I had no partner at the fair. I didn't know Nora's parts of the presentation. How was I supposed to learn that stuff tonight on top of everything else? There'd be no extra credit for being solo, either.

"Mol? What's wrong?" Max crouched down by my chair, his face full of worry.

"Nora's sick," I finally said.

Another crack of thunder cracked and Max looked terrified, but probably not about the weather. "Do you feel sick too?"

I shrugged.

"Holy moly. Maybe you should lie down, Molly. I need to call your parents."

Max thought I was sick like Nora. He was going to call Mom and Daddy and they would come rushing home. Wow. It was the hugest temptation to let him believe that. Being sick, especially pretend-sick, would make my stress go away. Max would send that girl right home and I could lie on the couch and eat crackers until my parents were back to take care of poor, sick Molly. Never mind about the State Fair. Nobody would be in the New Hampshire spot. It would be a big blank spot, and that would be fine with me.

But no. Even in the messy situation I was in, and with a really great alibi or excuse, I could not pretend to be sick. I just couldn't. It would be a big lie and make everyone around me full of worry. I hope that says something good about me. "No. I'm fine. But I need to go get Nora's project stuff."

"You sure?" Max looked relieved about the not-sick thing, like that was the most important thing of all.

The kitchen phone rang again. I answered it real quick, hoping it would be Mrs. Sutter saying she was only joking about Nora being sick.

"It's Hannah."

I felt some relief at the sound of her voice, even though I had forgotten all about the case for a while.

"I'm calling because I can't do the video thing for you tonight. Don't be mad. I told you I probably couldn't," she added real fast.

My hopes went swirling away. "Why not?"

"My brother is being a creep to me about using his stuff, for one thing. He locked it all up in his trunk. And my mom won't let me use hers either. Sorry, Molly. I did try."

"Nora's sick." I blurted this out, hoping it would change her mind or make her offer to help me in some other way, even though I didn't have any idea how.

"What kind?"

"Throw-up."

"Oh, that's horrible! Poor Nora!" Then Hannah did a big gasp. "Does that mean she'll miss the State Fair? Molly! What're you gonna do?"

"I have no idea. That's why —"

"Well, wow. That's horrible. But . . . but I really have to go now. I need to get to Kaylie's for pizza and to work on our. . . . Sorry, Molly," she said again. "Good luck tonight."

"Bye," I whispered, then slowly put the phone back where it belonged. My brain was in "stop" position. Tweets zoomed into the kitchen and landed on the window sill.

"Mol? Now what?" Max sounded like he had too much to deal with.

TAP! Tap tap tap.

"What's Paulie doing?" Sophie had followed Tweets into the kitchen. Seeing her again, as if they had not seen each other in a zillion years instead of only five minutes, made Max forget about everything else and look way too happy.

Nobody cared that my whole life was becoming a big mess. "Morse code," I said quietly, then headed for the back door, alone.

Chapter Nine
Nubb trouble

"Be careful crossing the street," Max called after me.

"Bye, Molly!"

"*Pretty, pretty, pretty!*"

I closed the door and headed away from my house, but not away from my stress. That went with me. A big, fat raindrop hit me on the nose and I wiped it away. Have you ever had a day go so bad on you? A day when everyone you needed to count on was totally not there for you?

If you have, I'm really sorry to hear that.

A person should never ask "what else can go wrong?" when that is how life is going, because that's exactly when something else bad happens. Daddy calls it Murphy's Law. Well, I forgot that law and asked that question as another raindrop hit me, this time splashing in my eye. "What else can go wrong?!"

I crossed the street carefully (like I always do), then had to dodge raindrops and also Nate Sutter's yard full of toys on my way to the front door. The Sutter's front door is a little bit creepy because there are spider webs and stuff. We use ours quite a bit, but theirs doesn't get opened much, except for Halloween. Everyone always goes in the garage door, but the garage was closed right now. The house was all sealed up to keep the germs inside.

The salt dough map was in a big pizza box on the porch. According to Nora it was totally fragile and whatever, so I had to be super careful with it. I took a peek under the cover. Mrs. Sutter had put a sheet of plastic wrap over the map, which I had to admit, was pretty cool. The state of New Hampshire had trees and mountains, a big blue lake, rivers and stuff. There were flags marking the important cities, rivers, mountains, etc. It looked like Nora and her mom had spent fifteen trillion hours on it, just like she had said.

I closed up the box after tucking the plastic wrap tightly over the map again, because it was raining a bit. I looked in the plastic grocery store bag that had been on top of the pizza box. There were two headbands, some beads, and other decorative things jangling around in there, plus a note for me. I stayed on the spider-webby porch for a few seconds to read it.

Molly,
There are headbands in the bag with state symbols to glue on. Wear that, plus the purple shirt.
Nora

Even when she was sick, Nora was bossy and mad at me. She could have at least said "thanks," couldn't she? I would've.

Rats. The rain was coming down harder now, not sprinkles, but the next step up. I could still make it, walking fast, but not running. I had to watch out for Nate's toys again, so I needed to watch my feet. I kept checking the box to be sure it wasn't tipping one way or another or getting too wet. And, of course, I checked the road. It was a lot to look at and think about.

A car drove by, almost splashing me with a puddle. I waited until it was way past me, then looked again — left, right, left.

And that's when the rain really started. I mean, it was like a gigantic bucket of water got dropped right on Taylor Drive. I have never gotten so wet so fast from rain. I protected the box the best I could but it was really hard. I prayed that it would only get the box wet, not the map. A wet map would be a disaster, for sure.

I finally crossed the street, after looking left, right, and left again and seeing no cars anywhere. I made it to the sidewalk in front of my house. The rain was making gigantic puddles, and it was hard to know where to step. Darn it! I was wearing my school shoes and they would be wrecked if I ended up in a deep puddle.

And then, believe it or not, things got worse.

He was coming fast, riding his bike right on the sidewalk, zooming right at me, a mean grin on his face, head down, water spraying all over from his tires. . . .

I could not believe it. He did not slow down or get out of my way. He kept coming at me with his head down, speeding up until I had to jump so I wouldn't get hit by the bike.

After I jumped, I lost my balance and started to fall.

And the pizza box flew out of my hands, landed on its side, and burst open. The map fell into a big puddle, then broke into pieces.

Chapter Ten
Everything is ruined

I stood in the noisy, crowded gym, all by myself between Nevada and New Jersey. But my project was incomplete without Nora's physical map. It was not interesting. It had no oomph. The lights from Nevada flashed in my eyes and called to the judges. No one voted for me. No one.

Mom and Daddy were disappointed and shocked, because they had expected much better from me.

Mrs. Kelly was sorry, but since there was no physical map, Nora and I got an F. The State Fair was so important to our grades that the F meant we did not pass 4th grade social studies. We both had to go to summer school.

Nora totally blamed me for the ruined map and the F in social studies, so she would not talk to me. And summer school lasted the whole entire summer (and was taught by a mean teacher).

Max and Sophie solved the mystery for Amelia, catching that mean Benny Nubb in the act and saving the day. Teddy and Pip decided that they loved Max, and loved Sophie even more. They were so mad at me for having summer school every day that they did not even want me to stop by anymore once it was done.

    Max and Sophie had a wedding in Amelia's living room, and the guinea pigs wore their hats. I was not even invited, but the grandmas were. All of them decided that they liked Sophie better than me too, since I had not written them any letters. Even Nanna, who is my related grandma.

    Everyone was disappointed in me, even me.
    I had failed.
    Everything.
    Everyone.

Chapter Eleven
Okay, that's not exactly what happened

"Mol? Molly? Are you okay?"

I blinked my eyes once, twice, three times, shaking myself out of the horrible awake-nightmare I had just had. I was sitting in the wet grass right in front of my house. Every inch of me was soaking wet or muddy. Or both.

Max waved his hand in front of my eyes, then snapped his fingers at me. "Molly?" He was all wet too, a total mess compared to before, and he was holding a squirming Benny Nubb by the arm. When did he get there?

"Lemme go!" Benny Nubb tried to get loose, but he couldn't get away from Max.

"How would you like it if someone ruined your homework the night before a big presentation-type-thing?" Max said. "Huh? How would you like it?"

"I didn't mean to do that," Benny mumbled, still squirming.

"It sure looked like you did," Max said. "You came right at her, didn't even swerve!"

"I would've, but she jumped!" Benny shouted it this time. "I didn't mean to wreck anything!"

"Then what *did* you mean to do? Huh? What did you think would happen, riding your bike really fast at someone like that when it's raining so hard?"

"She's been bugging me at school for, like, two days! Staring at me and spying on me!"

"Oh, so you're the one," Max said.

"The one, what?"

"The one who's bugging your next-door neighbors, keeping them up at night with your shenanigans. Amelia told me."

"Who's Amelia?"

"What is going on out here?!" Benny Nubb's mom had smelled trouble and appeared under a big black umbrella. "Benny? What have you gotten yourself into now? What is he saying about the next-door neighbors?"

"He won't let me go!" Benny wailed. "And I didn't do anything to those neighbors!"

Mrs. Nubb flicked her eyes all around. "The new neighbors? The nice professor and his wife? What else have you done, Benjamin? Why in the name of Pete would you . . . ?" Her eyes found the ruined map and got really big.

"He was riding his bike on the sidewalk, coming right at her," Max explained. "Molly lost her balance and her stuff got ruined. This was a big school project, due tomorrow."

Mrs. Nubb's eyes went from big to really tight.

"All we really want here is an apology." Max finally let his prisoner go and stood by me instead. "Then we need to get to work."

"I didn't mean to do it!" Benny Nubb repeated.

"Benjamin Nubb," his mother snapped, "the fact is, you *did* do it, and look at the mess! This girl will have to do a lot of extra work tonight because of your carelessness." She turned to me. "Molly, he will find a way to make this up to you. Benny? Where is that apology? I am not hearing one!"

"But I didn't mean to wreck anything, and I didn't do anything to those neighbors!" Benny wailed.

"Now!" his mother repeated.

"I didn't —"

"Alright, alright. If that's how it's gonna be – how about some time in your room, thinking about what you've done?" Mrs. Nubb grabbed his arm and started walking him down the sidewalk toward their house.

I could hear him defending himself over and over again.

But I didn't feel anything. I didn't care.

Max had gathered up the ruined map pieces and the pizza box. Maybe he thought there was a way to put it all back together again. There wasn't. It was all the way ruined – fifteen trillion hours of work. Humpty Dumpty had a great fall.

"Come on," he said, then led me to the porch. "Come on, Mol. Let's sit down."

I sat on the porch, a big, muddy mess.

"I'm really sorry, Molly," Max said, in a really nice way that made my eyes sting. "What a rotten thing to happen."

I did a little bitty nod.

"Rotten," he said again.

I nodded again.

"And . . . well. . . ." Max shook his head. "Rotten."

I sighed a little.

"But Mol, I mean, for what it's worth, I'm here. For you."

I swallowed.

"Tell me how I can help, okay?" He said it so nicely, and then he hugged me, mud and all.

And I fell apart into ten zillion wet pieces. Just like Nora's map.

Chapter Twelve
Molly Jane Fisher, the problem volcano

After I stopped being a crying faucet, I turned into a volcano with problems shooting out of my mouth like boiling hot lava, all over Max.

"And Mom was going to help me get letters ready for my Grandma Club for tomorrow," I said. The worst of the stuff I was upset about was out, and I was starting to calm down. Or at least to not be so darn hiccup-y. "But now there is no way I can get them done. I don't have time! And that means their feelings will be hurt, which is horrible. They count on me to write them letters, Max, and draw pictures for them that make them smile. I never show up at Shady Acres without something for each of them — never! Showing up with nothing in my hands makes it look like I don't think about them, but I do!

"I can't do anything right today, Max. Everything is horrible! My State Fair project is going to be the worst one out of fifty. I mean, how in the world can I make one of those maps in a big rush tonight, when it took Nora and her mom ten zillion hours to do that one?" I pointed at the map pieces with my foot.

Max said, "Um. . . ."

"But the project was boring even before the map got ruined. We had no ideas about how to make it more exciting. We worked so hard, for weeks and weeks, and now we aren't going to win any ribbons at all. I have no ideas, and I am so sick and tired of it! I don't want to work super-duper hard on it tonight and then be totally ignored by kid judges because we are stuck between show-off states."

Max said, "Uh . . ." this time, then, "well. . . ."

"Teddy and Pip asked me to either make their house safe or help them move out. That's how desperate they are, Max. Now they think someone else will be better help than me." I didn't say who. I did not want to talk about Sophie. "I don't even think they like me anymore." Uh oh. I slowly turned to look at Max after I said that secret-spilling stuff.

Max must have thought I was having a big imagination moment because he didn't look shocked or confused, only sorry for me. "Aw, I'm sure that's not true," he said. "Teddy and Pip are crazy about you, Mol."

"My friend Hannah lives right across the street from that boy and would be able to do the surveillance, but she said she couldn't." I did a big sigh. "I am a detective who doesn't give up on cases or totally fail at solving them. If I don't solve this one, nobody will trust me anymore, and I won't have any more cases."

"People won't think like that, Mol. You'll get more cases."

"Benny Nubb is tapping on their windows. You met him. You know what he's like, Max. He is so mean. But I can't get evidence, and he is going to get away with it." I covered my face with my hands. "And that is so unfair. His mom can't watch him all the time, Max." Oh my gosh, I felt tired after saying all that stuff, like I needed a nap instead of a whole long night of homework.

"We need to fix all of that tonight, huh?" When I looked at his face, Max actually looked a little scared. He fingered his cell phone.

"Yeah."

"Huh. Well . . . I mean. . . ."

"We're doomed. I mean, I am. You don't have to be."

Max reached out a hand and squeezed my shoulder. "No, you're not doomed. Or alone here. You've got me. Look. . . . Hey. Like I said, I'm here for you, kid. For what it's worth. Totally. Whatever I can do. Which, you know, won't be . . . um . . . I'm not exactly the most . . . the best . . . when it comes to school stuff. . . ." He took a deep breath. "You've got me. Okay? At your service."

"It's worth a lot, Max. I'm glad you're here," I said. "You were awesome with Benny Nubb, by the way."

Max shrugged and grinned about that. "He's not so tough."

"Thank you," I said, and I meant it all the way down to my toes.

Max and I smiled at each other. Then he said, "So, what now?"

"I have no idea."

We thought for a while after that. Finally, Max snapped his fingers. "I know where to start."

"Where?"

"We'll order a pizza," he said. "Everything works out better when a person is full of pizza. And then. . . ." Max's eyes slowly got big. "Oh my gosh. Oh no."

"What?"

"Sophie."

Oh yeah. Sophie.

He looked at his ruined outfit, then patted at his hair and groaned.

"It's probably best to take her home." I tried to sound sorry for him about that. "I mean, it won't be much fun for her around here, and we have a ton of stuff to do."

He did a little cough, then a nod. "Guess it wasn't meant to be," he said. "Tonight, I mean, with Sophie."

"Guess not." I was having a hard time looking at him now. Why did I feel bad? I had enough to feel bad about, didn't I? And she *should* go home. This was a terrible night.

"Okay. Well, I'll go find her," he said.

"Okay."

"What should I do with this?" Max asked, pointing the toe of his shoe at the pizza box.

"Garbage," I sighed.

The next time I saw him, Max looked a lot more like himself. Because he was wearing a pair of Daddy's sweatpants and a Yankees T-shirt. "Feeling a bit drier?" he asked. He opened the just-delivered pizza box and chose a steamy slice.

"I had to take a whole shower. That's how muddy I was," I said. "You found some of Daddy's clothes, huh?"

"Hope he doesn't mind." Max looked down at the new outfit. "Guess I'm not the type of dude to . . . you know . . . run around in white shirts, anyway."

We both chomped without talking as Tweets talked enough for all of us, chattering away about himself, flying from one perch to the next.

"*Birdie, birdie! Pretty, pretty! PRETTY BIRDIE!!!*"

"Um, Max?"

"Hmm?"

"Don't we have to . . . take her home?" It seemed weird that now Sophie was nowhere to be found.

"Uh, no, actually. We don't need to take her home."

His voice was so quiet that it made my insides tight as drums. "You mean, she's not leaving?"

"Opposite," he said with his mouth full.

"What does that mean?"

"*BIRDIE, BIRDIE, BIRDIE!*"

"When I got downstairs — you know, from cleaning up — she was already gone." Max shrugged like it was no big deal, but his face told me it kind of was a huge deal. "She left a note," he added. "She called up her mom and got a ride."

I picked up my pizza again. "Oh," was all I could think of to say about that.

Max filled his mouth up with pizza, probably because he didn't want to talk about this anymore.

"*HELLO? HELLO! BIRDIE, BIRDIE!*"

"Tweets, shh!" I said. "Show better judgment, please."

"So," Max said with his mouth full of food, "what should we tackle first?"

"*Pretty boy! Hello! Hello! Pretty birdie! BIRDIE, BIRDIE!*"

Somewhere in the back of my insides I felt guilty that Sophie was gone. I hadn't been nice, so she felt like she should leave. Worst of all, Max was sad, and it was my fault. "Maybe you can have a date tomorrow," I said real quiet.

"She's leaving tomorrow. She'll be gone for two weeks."

"Where's she going?"

"She's working at a summer camp — you know, with kids — for the whole summer. Tomorrow is the start of training."

"Oh."

"Her old boyfriend will be there."

"How old is he?"

Max did a little chuckle. "He isn't old, Mol. He's . . . previous."

"Oh."

"They broke up last weekend."

"Huh."

"So, being together at the training will probably be . . . no big deal. . . ." Max's voice got quieter and quieter.

"No big deal," I agreed.

"Except it's at a campground — the training. There'll probably be a lake and the moon and stars and stuff."

"Probably," I said slowly. "Unless it's cloudy or raining."

"Romantic stuff."

I frowned. "So?"

"He probably plays the guitar and cooks . . . and reads poetry to her. . . ."

"Well, he sounds totally weird to me, Max. Compared to you."

He pointed at my plate. "Eat! Then we need to make a plan."

"*HELLO??!!!!*"

"Tweets! Come on, shhh! I'm sorry, Max. About Sophie."

"What? Hey, nothing to be sorry about," he said, with another full mouth of food. "You are having a tough day, don't worry about my . . . about my stuff."

"I guess."

"Not meant to be, I suppose. I mean . . . her and me."

"*Hello! Hello! BIRDIE, BIRDIE! SCREEEEEECH!*"

"What's up with the bird?"

"I really have no idea."

"Should we let him join us?"

"He'll end up on your head, or mine," I said.

Max got a little smile about that, patted at his hair, and said, "Oh well. Whatever."

"His name is Tweets," I said, but Max had no reaction at all to that information. "Okay, I warned you. I'll let him out, and he'll end up on your head, probably, or the ceiling fan." But Tweets, just to make me look wrong, flew right to the window sill.

TAP! Tap tap tap.

TAP! Tap tap tap.
TAP! Tap tap tap.
Max watched him without saying anything.
"He's doing Morse code," I said.
"What's he saying?"
"That doesn't shock you?" I asked.
"Mol, nothing around here shocks me. You know that. What's he saying?"
"B."
"Like, a bumblebee?"
"No, like the letter B. That's what he always taps. B. Over and over again."
Max looked at me for a while, then said, "Huh."
"I think he is trying to help me solve the mystery."
Max nodded, shrugged, nodded.
"Or give me evidence, which is what I totally need, as you know. We all know the criminal is Benny Nubb."
Max nodded.
"Tweets is saying B, like the first letter in his first name and the last letter in his last name. Benny Nubb."
"Hmm."
"Don't you think?"
Max shrugged.
"Tweets must have seen!" I said. "Oh my gosh! Max! Tweets saw Benny Nubb doing his mischief at Amelia's house, and now he's trying to tell me!"
"But I don't think you can put Mr. Feathers on the witness stand," Max said.
"Yeah," I sighed. "I know. Darn it." Then something popped into my head. "You were supposed

to go over there tonight so Amelia could have quiet time to write."

"I'll call her up and tell her the situation. I'm sure she'll understand. We need to talk about homework," Max said.

"We'll both go over there," I offered. "I'll bring all my project stuff along and — oh my gosh."

"What?"

"Oh my gosh!"

Max set his pizza down, looking at me like I had gone cuckoo. "Mol? What?"

"Max! I have to make a physical map tonight!"

"Uh . . . yeah. I know. Let's get on that."

"But how?" I groaned, as Tweets landed on my head and screamed at me.

"*BIRDIE! BIRDIE! BIRDIE!!!!*"

I had no idea how to make a map like that. I hadn't had to know — it wasn't my part. All I knew was that Nora had complained or bragged all week about how much work it had been and how perfect hers turned out.

And I had to admit that it had turned out perfect. But now it was in the garbage.

Oh my gosh, she was going to be so super-duper mad at me, as if it was my fault that her map got ruined. Which was hardly fair. She probably wouldn't care that I had almost been run over by Benny Nubb and his bike. I put my hands over my face and groaned.

"First of all, don't worry about going to Amelia's house. The most important thing is to replace that broken map. And how we're going to do it is . . . give me a minute here. It'll come to me. Hang on." Max was quiet for a long time, then he snapped his fingers. "I'll call my mom."

I uncovered my face. "That's a pretty good idea. Moms always know stuff."

"I think maybe your friend exaggerated a bit about how hard it was, or how long it took to make that thing," Max went on, looking hopeful. "It'll probably be no big deal. Mom'll know how to do it." Max put his phone up to his ear. "No big deal," he repeated. "Piece of cake. Or dough. A piece of dough. That's all. Easy."

Tweets flew to the window, tapped another B, then landed on my head again.

"Map-making is Priority One." Max was making a different call, because nobody picked up the first time.

"Right," I mumbled. "Tweets, step up!"

"If we get a good start on the map by seven, then maybe we can pop over to Guinea Pig Central and help Amelia. Maybe. But only if it's going smoothly. I mean, there's no way a person can do any big thinking down there. Trust me, I tried. It's a no-go."

"Teddy and Pip won't be noisy tonight," I sighed. "They'd rather see Sophie than me. Plus, they're totally scared because they are so sure that the tapping sounds are scary monsters." I realized I had done a double slip-up: mentioning Sophie and also telling Max what Teddy and Pip were "thinking." I changed the subject back to Tweets. "It's past time to get off my head," I said, encouraging him to step up on a finger. "Step up, Tweets. Step up."

He flew to the window instead, taking some of my hair with him. *TAP! Tap tap tap.* "*Birdie! BIRDIE! HELLO?! HELLO?!!!!*"

"Tweets, don't be like that, or you're getting tucked in early."

Max set his phone down on the table and said, "Well, that figures."

"What? What figures?"

"My mom isn't picking up her phone. It's her bowling night."

"Aunt Patty has a bowling night?"

"*Birdie, birdie, birdie! Birdie, birdie, birdie! BIRDIE, BIRDIE, BIRDIE!!*"

"Tweets! Gee whiz!"

"*BIRDIE, BIRDIE, BIRDIE!!*"

What the heck was going on with Tweets? He had never been this crazy before. Never. I tried again to get him on my finger, but he kept on running away from me, pacing back and forth on the window sill.

"Mol? Plan B. Let's look up map-making on the computer, huh?" Max said.

"I need to get him in his cage. He's being cuckoo," I said.

"True. But we really need to get started." Max looked at his watch, then let out a puff of air. "Okay, you corral the parakeet, and I'll get started on your dad's computer," he said. "I'll do some surfing about maps made out of . . . ?"

"Salt dough," I said. "Okay. I'll be right there."

It took a while, but I finally got Tweets on my finger.

"*Birdie,*" he said, in a much more calm way. He looked right at me. Well, as right at me as a bird can, with their eyes on both sides of their head like they are. "*Birdie.*"

I petted his little yellow head with a finger. "You saw him, didn't you, Tweets? You saw him red-handed and are trying hard to tell me all about it."

"*Pretty, pretty birdie!*"

"I know. And I hear you. Thank you. I appreciate it so much." I gave him a kiss on his warm little beak. "You are a good boy and a good detective. I'll take it from here. You get some rest."

Tweets hopped in and went right to his water dish. He made a mess gulping it down. Then he went to his sleeping swing. He had to be worn out from all the detective work.

"Thanks, Tweets. I love you!"

Time to make a map.

Chapter Thirteen
Spilled beans

"*Max, where is the Sophie? Why is she not here at our house cuddly-cuddling with us right now? We want to do that thing! We love that girl and want her here. Thank you. Why are you also not here at our house, Max? We are waiting and waiting for you while monsters click and click at our windows, but there is no Max. And Amelia says to us that it is time for more diversion and turns on the computer TV. She goes to her upstairs room with that no-good celery phone - for minutes only, she says, but it has been much much more time than minutes! We look for Molly Jane, but instead we get Max on the computer TV!*"

"*WHERE IS MOLLY JANE?! DID MONSTERS CRUNCH HER?! TELL US THAT IS NOT THE NEW CARROT-ORY, MAX! CRUNCH CRUNCH CRUNCH! WHY IS THAT CLAW-FOOT BIRD SCREAMING AND SCREAMING, MAX?! WHERE IS MOLLY JANE?*"

"Dudes, calm down. First of all, Molly is fine. She's in the kitchen. And where are you two, by the way? Someplace really purple, it looks like."

"We are in the safe place called kitchen, same as Molly Jane, only different. There is no safe place in this monster house, but only the kitchen and our igloo, which is indeed a purple place. Monsters do not like kitchens, or purple, or —"

"CHICKEN TOWELS! DO NOT FORGET THOSE THINGS! CHICKENS ARE SCARY, MAX!"

"You mean a kitchen towel, right? Kitchen, not chicken."

"I MEAN WHAT I MEAN, AND I SAY CHICKEN!"

"What's a chicken towel?"

"Never mind that, Max. Why are you not here? Why are you on Molly Jane's computer TV instead of here?"

"We're kinda having a situation here."

"'Situation' is not what we want to hear about, Max. We have enough situation here in our haunted no-good house. We need for you to be here and to fight monsters with your sword and shield, dude! Thank you."

"My sword and shield?" Max laughed.

"Go, Max, go!"

"YOU CAN DO IT IF YOU TRY!"

"Don't get your little-dude hopes up about what I can help you with. I can't seem to do much of anything for anyone tonight."

"DO NOT SAY THINGS LIKE THAT! MAX IS A DUDE WHO EATS DUDE FOOD! MAX CAN FIGHT OFF CLICKETY MONSTERS! MAX TO THE RESCUE! WHERE IS THE PRETTY AND SMART SOPHIE?!"

"Um. . . ."

"*DO NOT SAY UM! WHERE IS SHE?*"

"She went home. She had to . . . do stuff. Tonight."

"*WHAT DID YOU DO WRONG?!*"

"*Did you call her 'dude'? Did you make her eat dude food? Did she see you in those clothes with that hair?*"

"Worse. She left without any dinner. It didn't turn out to be much of a date. I mean, it wasn't a date at all. But I did make plans — careful ones that you guys would've totally liked: a restaurant with cloths on the table and everything. But then. . . ."

"*Amelia asks for your help in saving us from monsters,*" Teddy said quietly. "*Sorry, Max.*"

"Don't get me wrong, dudes. I was glad to help out. I mean, I still am, if I can. I thought Sophie was okay with it, but . . ." Max trailed off. "Anyway, then Aunt Jane called up, freaking out —"

"*MAX, DO NOT SPEAK OF MOM JANE TO US, PLEASE! ALWAYS SHE IS FREAKING OUT AND BRINGING WORST OF TIMES BY PUTTING US IN BUCKETS!*"

"I needed to be in three places all at the same time tonight. I thought I could make everyone happy. But as it turns out —"

"*NO ONE IS HAPPY, DUDE!*"

"*Max, what is it that you are wearing? You do not look right. We told you and told you about the right things to wear for the dating, and still you do not listen! You are slop-slop-sloppy, and the hair is all wrong.*"

"Little dudes, do not go there with me now, okay? You have no idea what sort of a time I'm having here. And, by the way, I was totally dressed up before, like in a way you totally would've approved of. I even got a haircut."

"GOOD JOB, MAX! GOOD JOB, DUDE!"

"What happened to make you look no good? You look like our Wally dresses for fixing a toilet. P.U.!"

"WE LIKE THE SOPHIE! WHERE IS SHE? DO NOT FIX TOILETS AROUND THE PRETTY AND SMART SOPHIE, MAX! GIRLS DO NOT LIKE THAT THING!"

"You two were there on Sunday, listening in and totally spying on us. I mean, did it seem to you that she kinda did . . . like me? Sort of? A little? In spite of everything that went wrong? That always seems to go wrong?" Max sighed.

"*Max, we told you that answer already. Why would it be different than it was?*"

"Then why did she leave like that without even talking to me first?"

"HOW CAN WE KNOW THAT, MAX? YOU SILLY! WE ARE HERE, NOT THERE!"

"She's going to a camp counselor training tomorrow, and her old boyfriend will be there."

"*Max, the part about old boyfriend is still true too. Do not worry your messy head. Yes, it is true that you are a strange dude with no romantic in you, but the Sophie does not want to do the dating with that guy. He only made her mad, madder, and maddest. Remember that thing? Pip and me saved the day for you, and so don't waste it! Do not be the thing of ridiculous or forget all of our important lessons!*"

"*DUDE! WE WASTED OUR TIME ON YOU TIME AND AGAIN! DON'T MAKE US MAD!*"

"Dudes, come on!" Max laughed a little.

"*No, Max, you come on!*" Teddy giggled.

"*DUDE!!!!*"

"*The Sophie is not liking of him. It is something else that is wrong. Tell me what you did to make her go away. Besides the no dinner, the sloppy clothes, and messy hair.*"

"Aw, I don't know. It was a bunch of crazy stuff, not one thing. You know? That kid, Nubb, and the map, and —"

"*NO MAPS! DO NOT SPEAK OF MAPS OR MOM JANE! OR BUCKETS OR ELEPHANTS OR —*"

"The truth is, I don't know why she left. I got into a situation here with Molly, and she needed me the most just then, and when that was sort of calmed down, Sophie was gone. Sorry, guys, I really hoped to be able to stop by, but I'm not sure if I can now. See, Molly has to remake a map now for her —"

"*AGAIN YOU SAY 'MAP' TO PIP?! DO NOT TALK OF MAPS, MAX! WORST OF ALL TIMES! SHHH! STOP THAT!*"

"Sorry, Pipster. Whatcha got against those things, anyway?"

"*Max, do not try to understand Pip. He is some crazy, especially about maps.*"

"*DO NOT TALK AGAIN AND AGAIN ABOUT THOSE THINGS! I AM NOT CRAZY!*"

"Anyway, that kid, Nubb, made her fall in the rain and the . . . uh . . . thing we won't mention, that her friend Nora had already made, got wrecked, and now she needs another one for tomorrow."

"*Is our best friend Molly Jane alright?*" Teddy squeaked. "*Neighbor boy of Nubb makes her fall?*"

"*NOOOOO GOOOOOOOD!*"

"*It sounds to me that Molly Jane is having a day that gets badder and baddest.*"

"You got that right, Teddy."

"*Max, you take care of our Molly Jane, okay? We will be alright, for a time, in this purple igloo in the chicken-towel kitchen. I hope. When you are finished saving Molly Jane's day, then come over to this haunted monster house and take care of the monsters, too. Okay? You can do it. We have much believing in you, Max.*"

Max chuckled. "Okay, buddy. I'm on it."

"*Bring the Sophie, okay? She will still be liking Teddy and Pip, even if she is hungry and not liking your slop-slop-sloppy clothes and hair. Uh oh. Pip, shhh! Uh oh! Beans! Beans!*"

"*WHAT?! UH OH! SHHH!*"

"What's up, Pipster? Teddy?" Max slowly turned around until our eyes locked together.

Chapter Fourteen
Best friends all together

Daddy's office went quiet, and all three guys stared at me. Busted.

Pip whispered one more "*UH OH,*" then hid behind Teddy in the igloo.

After a few seconds, they both peeked out and started making guinea pig sounds.

"*Whoop whoop whoop!*"

"*WHEEEEEEEEEEK! WHEEEEEEEEEEK!*"

"I heard you guys," I said. "So never mind with that."

"*TOAST!*" Pip whispered.

"Yeah. Toast." So, there it was. This was why the guys had said nice things about Max, or at least not said anything bad since I got back from Florida. Teddy and Pip not only liked Max now, they were talking to him. They had talked to him last weekend, letting him in on the biggest secret ever. They had trusted him and broke the biggest rule of all.

I sank onto the floor, feeling confused. I had had way too many feelings today and was starting to be exhausted from all of it.

"Uh, look, Mol. . . ." Max started waving his hands in front of him. But he couldn't come up with the right words. And that made sense, I suppose. I mean, it is not something that is easy to come up with the right words about. Talking guinea pigs, big secrets.

"*Don't tell Amelia!*" Teddy finally squeaked. "*Please, Molly Jane? She does not know this thing. Plus, it was Pip who spilled the beans, not Teddy, and so it is not my fault.*"

"*OBJECTION!*"

"*Pip was doing singing in the telly-phone to our Amelia, and Max heard this, and then there were beans everywhere!*"

"NO, NO, NO! NOT BEANS! NO BEANS! PIP SAVED THE DAY!"

Max and I looked at each other for a long, quiet while.

"*Please, Molly Jane?*" Teddy asked again.

"I won't tell Amelia," I finally said. "But I don't like having a secret from her. About a secret. It's getting complicated."

"*DON'T TELL WALLY EITHER, MOLLY JANE!*"

"Or Wally," I sighed.

"*Or anyone! The web is tangly and webby. We know this thing. But —*"

"SHHH! DON'T TELL!"

"Guys, don't worry. I won't tell anyone. You can trust me."

"And me," Max said.

"How did . . . ? What happened last weekend?" I asked.

Max let out a long sigh. "I overheard Pip singing. Mol, I thought I was losing my mind, for real. Like, whoa. Then I caught Teddy talking on the phone to Amelia. Like, you know, complaining about me."

"*Teddy did not do that thing. No complaining was done. Or was it? Tee hee!*"

"*PIP IS A ROCK STAR!*"

"Did it freak you out?"

Max laughed. "What do you think? Yeah. Totally."

I giggled as I tried to imagine the whole thing, then giggled more. It actually felt great to do that.

"Yeah, real funny," Max said. "Thanks for your support."

"When I heard them the first time, I fell over on my butt. For real. I thought I was crazy. Or asleep."

"*NO GOOD!*"

Max laughed, then said, "It might've been nice if I'd known about this going into the gig." He raised his eyebrows up at me. "I had quite the time from Friday morning until Saturday night, with these two and their shenanigans. I have a feeling if I'd known the whole scoop, the shenanigans might've been less shenaniganny."

"*We did much and many jokes and tricks! Tee hee!*"

"*MUCH FUN AND FUNNY! BEST OF TIMES!*"

"One of these two got an apple core up and over that ledge and tossed it right at my head!"

"*PIP DID IT! TEE HEE!*"

"Almost knocked over one of Amelia's doodads, too. I made this amazing save —"

"Which one?" I asked, suddenly sitting up straight. "Was it a statue of a girl with an umbrella?"

"Yeah, and I made this amazing save —"

"Oh my gosh! Where is it, Max? What happened to it?"

"After my amazing save," Max paused, waited for someone to acknowledge his amazing save, then rolled his eyes, sighed, and said, "I tucked it away in the guest bedroom, on the dresser, to keep it safe. Why?"

"Amelia was wondering where that was. That's why. We just solved a mystery!"

"Well, anyway, these two were trying their hardest to get rid of me, but it didn't work. I hung in there, didn't I?"

"*We had to save the Sophie from weirdo stalker Max!*"

"*IT WAS WORST OF TIMES! WE WERE IN DANGER OF THE JAIL AND DOING TIME!*"

"You *what*?" I laughed.

Pip said, "*TEE HEE! THAT WAS A JOKE, MOLLY JANE!*"

"I'm sorry I couldn't tell you, Max. It's a huge secret. Huger than huge. Think about it, okay? If anyone knew, if scientists or the government found out —"

"*WE DO NOT WANT TO DO RESEARCH! I AM NOT WEARING A WHITE COAT! I AM A ROCK STAR! WE TOLD YOU THIS THING, MAX!*"

"*Do not call the science people or the FBI or ABC or CSI!*"

"Guys, come on! Seriously? We went over this, and you know I would never," Max said.

"*Yes, Max. We know that thing,*" Teddy said.

"What I'd like to know," Max said slowly, "is how and why these guys decided I was a rotten guy before they ever met me. What'd you say to them?"

"It wasn't me!" I said real fast. "No way! It was —"

"*MAX IS NO GOOD! TEE HEE! WE KNOW AND WE KNEW!*"

"*Sorry, Max. I will say it: we were wrong, mostly. But you did not do everything the right way. You do know that, right?*"

Max shook his head. "We have to be careful to keep the secret safe. All of us."

"*It was Pip who spilled those beans, not Teddy.*"

"*OBJECTION!*"

"You know, though, Mol, it's a pretty big relief that you and I can talk about this – about them – about you guys," he said, looking at them. "'Cuz honestly, it's quite a big thing to have to keep all to yourself."

"No kidding. Welcome to my world."

"It's nice to be able to let someone know that I know."

"Yes. Someone who thinks it's cool, not freaky. Now tell me the story of last weekend."

"*PIP SAVED THE DAY!*"

"*Let me tell! Let me! Teddy will tell the truth!*"

"Okay, Teddy, buddy, but I'm right here to fill in the gray areas," Max said.

"*OBJECTION!*"

"*There was a time, some time ago, when all best friends left poor guinea pigs alone in the* haunted house. The house was not haunted just yet, but we made it haunted with our jokes and tricks. Tee hee!"

"TEE HEE!"

Max shook his head, but he was smiling.

"The good and big plan was to make Max go away, but only after our Wally came back. Max did not do things right. He did not read Potter or do anything else right. Or enough."

"I turned on your TV and fed you."

"SHH! DO NOT STOP THE STORY, MAX!"

"So the smart guinea pigs did jokes and tricks with some 'psst' and some ghostly sounding sounds about 'we don't like you,' and also made some messes for Max to clean up – which was good for him. And also did noisy noises when he was talking on the phones."

Pip did a siren sound to demonstrate.

"They did that when I was trying to call Sophie for the first time," Max said. "She thought I was a weirdo." His smile got a little droopy, then he said, "Still does, I guess."

"*Max, you are a weirdo! Plus you are slop-slop sloppy! Tee hee hee hee!*"

"Thanks, Teddy."

"Anyway, that was the plan — the two plans, or maybe three: ghostly sounds, big noises, and messy messes. But Max did not go away. There was a time when he did a bad thing and blocked and trapped poor guinea pigs out of the walking path with no-good books . . ."

"PIP DID NOT DO HIS POTTY ON THAT BOOK!"

". . . and he went to the sleeping room and slept for days and days. But after the beans were spilled, we helped with the studies and taught him how to be a good date. But when it was time to do it, he did not listen and did it all wrong. And that was the end. Except the Sophie likes Teddy and Pip better than that Max. Apparently."

"PIP SAVED THE DAY!"

"I'll tell you the rest of it some other time," Max said. "Teddy might've left out a detail or two."

"The 'rest of it' maybe hurts my feelings," Teddy said. "Maybe it sounds like Max is telling Molly Jane that there is more to the story to be telling, and perhaps I did not tell the truly-truth!"

"DO NOT MAKE US MAD, MAX!"

"No offense, dudes. Anyway," he said, looking at all of us, "this is our secret — us four, right? We won't let Amelia or the professor know that I know, so you dudes don't get in trouble, but we can talk when it's just the four of us. Which is pretty darn cool."

"Uh oh! Amelia is coming! Shhh! Shhh! No more beans!"

Teddy and Pip stopped talking, and Max closed the laptop. "Well," he said, "there you go."

"There you go," I agreed, smiling. I couldn't believe I was smiling. What a weird day.

"Let's get that map going," Max said, picking up his piece of pizza. It had left a greasy spot on the desk and he wiped it up with a sleeve.

The doorbell rang before I could say how much I didn't want to make a map, talk about a map, or have anything to do with a map at all that night. I was totally on Pip's side about "maps are no good," actually.

"Maybe it's that kid, Nubb, coming by to apologize," Max said.

"Oh no! That is the last thing I need!" I said.

Max took a chomp of the pizza in his hand then opened the door.

Then his eyes got real big.

Then he dropped his pizza on the floor.

Why? Because it wasn't Benny Nubb at the door. It was Sophie.

Chapter Fifteen
Sophie is back, and Tweets is cuckoo

Max finally said, "Hi," and picked up the pizza. Then he just stood there. He didn't even ask her to come in, even though it was still raining. Sophie didn't seem to mind Max's weird manners and that he was being a statue. Or that he wasn't offering to help with the stuff she was carrying. She said hi too, then they both stood there, smiling at each other in the doorway (weird, huh?).

I did a little cough to unfreeze them, because we totally didn't have time for this.

Max remembered how to move and talk and said, "Oh! Hey. You're getting wet. And . . . you have . . . stuff. I mean, can I take something . . . ? Or . . . I mean, help you with . . . any of that?" He reached out to take something from her, remembered he had pizza in his hand, then stared at it like he had no idea how it got there or what to do with it.

"It's okay, I've got it," Sophie said with a little giggle. "And I know you two are really busy tonight, so I'll be quick."

"Be . . . quick? But. . . ."

"I mean, I won't stay long."

Max's dopey smile disappeared. "You won't?"

Sophie did a little shrug, then looked at me. "I had an idea – about your project."

Now it was my turn to stand there looking dumb.

"You . . . ? Molly's project? Idea? Wow! What? Really?" Max could only seem to say one or two-word sentences now that Sophie was at the door. And, apparently, he wasn't sure if he should smile or not. The in-between thing he was doing looked goofy.

Sophie looked at me. "I'm studying to be a teacher, and sometimes I get ideas. Like, they just hit me, you know?"

I knew how that went, usually. Not lately, though. Definitely not tonight.

"That is so — that is awesome. You came back — to help Molly." Max turned to look at me. "She has an idea. About your project."

I nodded as Sophie asked, "Do you mind if I step inside?"

"Huh? Oh! Right! Of course. Sorry. You're getting wet! Come in." When Max finally moved away from the door, he stepped right in pizza sauce. "Oh," he said. He lifted up his foot then stared at it. "Huh." He took off his sock, then stood there with it in his hand. "I should . . . I mean, I shouldn't . . . can't get pizza on . . . on Aunt Jane's carpet. We were having pizza, Molly and me." Max cleared his throat. "I'll be right back."

"*BIRDIE, BIRDIE, BIRDIE, BIRDIE, BIRDIE!!!*" Tweets screamed from the kitchen.

"Oh my goodness!" Sophie said, smiling toward the sound.

"Sorry about him," I said. "He's totally cuckoo today."

"Oh, Paulie is a sweetie," she said. "He isn't bothering me one bit."

I looked at her smile and her nice eyes. It didn't make sense that she was back, with ideas for me and a bag of stuff. But she was.

She slipped off her shoes.

"You can put your things down in here," I said, then led her to the living room. "Did you really think up an idea for my State Fair project?" I asked. *Even though I wasn't one bit nice to you when we met?* I didn't say that part; I just thought it in my head, feeling horrible about it. We sat across from each other with the coffee table between us.

"It popped right into my head," she said with a shrug. "It happens."

"And then you got . . . stuff . . . for the idea?" I added, the guilt heavier.

She held up her hands. "First of all, you don't have to hear or use my idea. You really don't. Like I said, it was something that popped into my head, but —"

"Sophie?" I interrupted, because her niceness was really giving me a guilty stomachache now. "I would really love to hear about it," I whispered. "Thanks."

"Okay. You're sure?"

I nodded. "I can't think straight tonight."

"Understandably," she said.

"That's why I haven't been very . . . me. Or very nice. Usually I am. Nice, I mean. And me."

When I looked up I saw that her smile was real and warm. "I have had a day or two like that too, Molly. I know what you mean."

"You have? You do?"

She laughed a little. "Of course. In fact, just last weekend . . . and then Max . . ." Sophie let the thought float away, her eyes going to the hallway where Max was tromping around in his bare feet. He gave her a goofy grin then wiped up the floor. "Anyway," Sophie said.

"Anyway," I shrugged.

"Here goes. Let's see what you think." She started taking things out of the big white shopping bag. This is what she lined up on the coffee table:

Three rolls of already-made sugar cookie dough
Cookie cutters (tons of them)
Tubes of frosting (in lots of colors)
Decorative sprinkles and candy
Post-it notes

Huh.

"You don't have to use this stuff or the idea," she said again.

I guess the stress was freezing my brain up, because I didn't see how cookies would fix my messed-up project. "Baking cookies?" I asked.

"Baking one cookie," she said, then waited for me to get it.

"One cookie?" That made even less sense to me. "Sorry, I don't —"

"I know it was snoopy of me, but I looked at your projects requirements." She said it like it was a terrible crime to do that. "They were on the kitchen table."

"What did it say about cookies?" I really did not care one bit if she read those things, or every scrap of my homework papers.

"What gave me the idea is what it didn't say."

"Um...."

"The physical map doesn't have to be made of *salt dough*," she said, saying the last two words slow and separate.

"Uh huh...?"

"It has to be a physical map — to show topography. That was the requirement. So unless your teacher specifically said that it had to be salt dough...?"

I scrunched up my brain, trying to remember. "I don't think so."

Outside, the rain got harder. I could heard thunder, the far-off rumbly kind. I looked from her to the stuff on the coffee table and then a light bulb finally clicked on and I understood. Not salt dough – cookie dough.

"A cookie map!"

Sophie smiled. "Different, and quicker to make, too. What do you think?"

I felt a smile on my face.

Sophie looked even happier than I was. "Do you like the idea?"

"Yes! I do!"

"You'll need to figure out how to shape it into New Hampshire. That's the only cookie cutter we didn't have at my house," she laughed. "Actually,

Mom probably has one, but not a huge one. Sorry, I didn't have time to figure that part out."

"I know how to do that." Max said that. Like, with a shrug and a "no big deal" look on his face.

"You?"

Sophie smiled at him with big eyes.

"Mom had to make a big cookie for that baby shower, that one time. It was shaped like a . . . a . . . baby buggy. But it could be anything." Max started to look a little bit embarrassed, like maybe it wasn't cool for a guy to know about large baby buggy cookies. He smoothed at his hair and did a little cough.

"How did you do it, Max?" I asked, shaking my head in amazement at that guy.

"Do what?"

"The giant cookie cutter. How did you do it?"

"Oh. That. Right. How did I do it?" There was that dopey grin again.

I waved a hand in front of his eyes and he blinked.

"What?"

"How did you make the giant cookie cutter?"

"Aluminum foil," he said. "I folded up aluminum foil, like, folded it up lots of times until it was thin but . . . I don't know . . . sturdy. Then we shaped it over a picture. A drawing of a . . . of that baby buggy. Most people have that. I bet. In the kitchen. Aluminum foil, not baby buggies." Max shrugged, then grinned at Sophie some more.

There was a flash of lightning; then, five seconds later – *BOOM!*

"We have aluminum foil," I said.

And Max said, "Awesome."

"The mountains and rivers could be done with frosting," Sophie said, turning her grin toward me and pointing to the tubes of different colors. "After it cools, of course."

"Yeah," I said. "'Cuz otherwise the mountains would melt into mud puddles."

"We actually might want to find a way to chill it." Sophie tapped on her chin. "Is there room in your refrigerator?"

The storm was closing in on us. Lighting. Thunder. *BOOM!*

Max, who was an expert at checking refrigerators, said, "I'm sure if we move some stuff around, it'd fit," then headed for the kitchen to take care of it.

"Thank you," I said, looking right into Sophie's green eyes and meaning it with all of my heart. "Thank you so much."

"I wish you all kinds of luck, Molly, and I hope it goes well for you tomorrow."

"Thanks. Today was one of my most unlucky days, like, ever. I'll need all the good luck I can get."

Max was back, holding a plate of leftover meatloaf from last night's dinner.

Sophie said, "I really wish I could stop by tomorrow and see how it all turns out."

"Me too," I said. "I mean, I wish *you* could. I don't have a choice about being there."

"Maybe you could take pictures for me?" Sophie asked Max.

"Yeah. Sure," Max said, his eyes dreamy. "Pictures."

"Could you send them to my phone?"

He nodded, stabbed the meatloaf with a fork, and took a bite.

"So . . . ?" Sophie said.

"So . . . ?" Max copied her.

"You can handle all of this, right?"

Max's dreamy eyes got blinky. "What? Who, me? Handle all this? Me? You're leaving? Already?"

"I don't want to intrude. You two have a lot to do."

Everything got super quiet for a while, except for another crack of thunder and Tweets shrieking his head off in the kitchen. "*BIRDIE! BIRDIE! BIRDIE! HELLO?!*"

Max moved his mouth but couldn't seem to make any words come out. He didn't seem to know what to do with the plate of meatloaf he was holding now.

She couldn't leave! We needed her! I blurted out, "Could you stay? Please?"

"*Pretty, pretty, pretty!*"

"Pretty please?" I added.

Sophie's eyes got sparkly, her smile wider. "I was really hoping you'd ask," she said. "The answer is yes!"

Sophie and I went right to work on the map as the weather went from crazy to crazier outside. I worried about Teddy and Pip in the background of my brain. I really, really hoped they weren't too scared. But of course they were. I knew that.

I couldn't think about it now, had to keep my focus on New Hampshire.

After Max put the meatloaf back in the fridge, he started cleaning. Like, kind of a weird amount of cleaning. He rinsed the muddy clothes, his and mine, wiped up the floor again, and then took the trash right outside to the garbage can. I had never seen him do anything like that before.

"You don't have to do that," I called after him, because he was totally going outside in the crazy rain. "Daddy always does that on Monday nights!" But he did it anyway. Weird.

"*Birdie, birdie, birdie! Birdie, birdie, birdie! BIRDIE, BIRDIE, BIRDIE!!*"

"He's usually not like this," I said to Sophie. "He can't seem to control himself tonight." Then I realized that I could have been talking about Max or Tweets when I said that. She must've thought I was talking about Max, because it made her cheeks a little bit pink and she looked away. I could tell she was smiling. I pulled the cloth over Tweets's cage so maybe he would quiet down and go to sleep. I did another "shh," then said "good night" to him. "I'll take care of it, Tweets," I whispered. "I promise. I love you. Get some rest! Never mind about those noises outside, okay?"

When Tweets was all tucked in, Sophie and I really got to work on that cookie map.

"I sure hope Teddy and Pip are okay," I said later, as I dug through the bag of stuff Nora had sent over. Where was the glue gun? I needed that thing. "They're afraid of . . . stuff. Especially tonight." I looked out the window for a bit, then turned away.

They didn't like noisy storms. Poor Amelia had her hands full right now.

"Max and I were going to spend some time with those two tonight," Sophie said. "I guess they have been a little noisy, and Amelia has a hard time writing. It is so cool that she is a writer – and lives two doors down from you! And is your friend!"

"She used to live right there in the garage apartment."

"Really?" Sophie's eyes got big.

"We've been through a lot together, all of us," I said. "I don't think much about her being famous. Sometimes I forget all about it. Right now, all I can think of is that she is having a hard time." I stopped my words in those tracks and thought, *who isn't?*

Nora had throw-up sickness, plus tight teeth. What a terrible combination! Also, she had to be disappointed about missing the fair after working fifteen trillion hours on the project, and probably felt bad because of all the fighting we were doing. Maybe she thought we weren't friends anymore, just like I had thought, after all those years of being best friends. And she wished it wasn't true, just like I did.

The more I thought about it, the more it seemed like everyone around me was having a hard time. Including Max and Sophie, not having their date tonight. She had to leave tomorrow for two weeks, and he was going to miss her. And maybe she was going to miss him, too, if I was reading her mind in the right way. She didn't want to spend two weeks with some weird guy who played poetry on his guitar in the moonlight. She liked Max.

And Amelia missed Wally so much, and he missed her.

And of course there were Teddy and Pip's big worries.

Even Mom and Daddy had something hard tonight. They had to rush downtown for a probably really boring dinner, so Daddy was missing his relaxing time, like a baseball game on TV, and Mom wanted to be here to help me. I'm sure she had seventeen other things she had hoped to do tonight, too.

Mrs. Sutter was home with two sick kids, and she was probably worried that she would get sick too. That is not an easy thing to have going on.

All the fourth graders were probably freaking out just as bad as me about the fair tomorrow. Well, all except the show-offs who thought they had the ribbon in their bag, no problem.

And my grandmas had hard times a lot of the time. They would be hoping for something special and exciting tomorrow. They liked to see me, plus have something to hold on to until I came back again — something to show them that I thought about them more than just when I was there.

I looked at Sophie, who came back here to help me, just because she was nice. She liked helping people, even me in my grouchy mood. And then something clicked into place in my brain.

Lightning. Thunder. *BOOM!*

"Molly?" Sophie tilted her head at me, probably because I was smiling now, kind of a lot.

"*BIRDIE!!!!!*"

Oh yeah, and then there was Tweets and his problems.

I jumped up from my chair, still smiling, then left the table and pulled open the crafts drawer. "I am going to make Nora a get-well card," I said, then grabbed light purple paper, guinea pig stickers, and my glue pens.

"That's a nice idea," Sophie said.

"What's up?" Max popped back into the kitchen. "What can I help with?"

"I'm going to make Nora a really great card, then I am bringing it to her house and we are going to be friends again," I said. "Then I totally need to practice my presentation so we win a ribbon tomorrow, and make those headbands, too. But I can do that stuff at Teddy and Pip's. Those two are probably scared of the storm right now, and we need to go over there so Amelia can go write. Right?"

"Right!" Max did a salute.

"Then I need to do something really special for the Grandma Club. And maybe something for Mom and Daddy, too."

"Geez, Mol, you're biting off an awful lot."

"I need to learn Nora's part of the presentation now, too. But I am not going to let that freak me out. No way," I said.

Max got a mysterious look on his face as Sophie started packing things up in her big bag. "Maybe you won't have to learn her part."

"Why not? Are you going to come to the fair tomorrow and pretend to be Nora?"

"I mean, maybe she doesn't have to totally miss the fair."

"Max? What are you talking about?"

But he just stood there, tapping his fingers on the counter and thinking his own thoughts.

"Max?" I waved a hand in front of his face.

"I have an idea for your project too," he finally said. "But I can't tell you yet. Can you hang in there while I think it through?"

"Can I ever!" I hugged that guy really tight.

"Go ahead and finish up that card, okay? I'll bring it over there for you when it's done," Max said, hugging back. "Make it awesome. I'll call Amelia and tell her we're all coming over."

"I have another idea!" I suddenly shouted, which made Tweets freak out again.

"BIRDIE! Birdie, birdie, birdie! Hello? Pretty birdie! Pretty BIRDIE! Birdie, birdie, birdie! Birdie, birdie, birdie! BIRDIE, BIRDIE, BIRDIE!!"

"What is it, Mol?" Max asked, laughing at the sudden crazy I had made happen.

"Actually, I have two! And you have to hang in there while I think it through," I laughed, then gave Sophie a secret look, because I was totally going to tell her everything as soon as Max left.

Tweets kept up the noisy talk while I finished Nora's card and told Sophie the two great ideas that had popped into my head. "I think good ideas come when you stop thinking so hard about your problems," I said. "At least that's what happened here tonight, for me."

Sophie said, "Yes. I think that's true."

"That's why you have good ideas, right?" I asked. "Because you don't spend your time thinking all about yourself?"

Sophie only smiled and said, "I love your ideas. I think. . . ." She tapped on her lip. "I think I'll run out and get some materials when Max is back, if you don't mind. Maybe I'll run to my house again and —"

"If I don't mind?" I shook my head at her and we both smiled. "That would be so nice."

"*Pretty BIRDIE! Birdie, BIRDIE, BIRDIE!!!*" Tweets took a few birdie breaths, then calmly said, "*Birdie.*"

I didn't, but Sophie totally fell for Tweets's guilty tripping, and she opened up his door. "Just for a minute," she said. "Everybody with green and yellow feathers gets some attention now!" She held out a finger. "Come on out, Paulie! Come on out, sweetie! Pretty birdie! Pretty boy!"

But Tweets didn't actually want attention; he wanted the case solved. He wanted Benny Nubb to be busted. How did I know that? Because he flew right to the window sill and started up Morse code: the letter B.

Chapter Sixteen
Riding the storm out

Rain rain rain rain,
Rain-rain — GO AWAY!
Rain rain rain rain,
I don't like you so GO AWAY!

Boom boom boom boom!
Boom-boom — STOP THE BOOM!
Boom boom boom boom!
I don't like you so GO TO YOUR ROOM!

Click click click click,
Monsters, GO AWAY!
Click click click click,
I don't like you so STAY AWAY!

"It's okay, Pip," I said. *Flash! Crack! Pounding rain.* . . . "It's okay. It's okay. I'm here, and Max is here, so you're okay." I held him real carefully in my arms, the chicken towel wrapped around him for extra safety. I paced around and around Wally and Amelia's little kitchen as the weather got stormier and stormier, the little room darker and darker. "It's okay, best friend Pip."

There wasn't a lot of room to pace around in that kitchen, but Max paced Teddy around too and tried not to run into me and Pip. "Hang in there, little buddy," he said. "It's only nature outside. It's nature being noisy. Nothing scary. Nothing to worry about."

"*BUT WALLY SAYS THAT THAT NOISE OUT THERE IS ABOUT BOWLING, MAX, NOT NOISY NATURE! BOWLING IS ABOUT HEAVY ROLLING BALLS, AND SO WHY DO YOU SAY OUR BEST FRIEND WALLY IS LYING?*" Pip squeaked.

Max said, "Uh . . ." then looked at me for help.

I shrugged.

"*IT IS NOT A GOOD TIME OR DAY FOR JOKES AND TRICKS, MAX!*"

"*When will the Sophie be back?*" Teddy asked. "*Surely she is not safe out there, Max! There are monsters and also heavy bowling balls, maybe. And oh no! What about our Amelia? Surely she is out there too! Oh no!*"

"Aw, no, little dude. Amelia is at the library, remember? It's really safe there, 'cuz if there's one place monsters steer clear of, it's libraries."

"*Is that true, Molly Jane?*"

I nodded.

"*WHY DO THE MONSTERS NOT LIKE LIBRARIES, MAX?!*"

"Well, 'cuz, you know . . . 'cuz they can't read," Max said.

"*Many many books and books and books make them mad and madder? Or maybe sadder?*"

"Uh huh. Yep. Right. And Sophie . . . she'll be quick." Max sounded a little worried about her, actually. "She'll be fine. I mean, she is fine."

"*Monsters and bowling balls won't get her?*" Teddy whispered. "*When the Sophie comes to this haunted house she won't get clicked by monster fingers?!*"

"Nah. No way. Know why?"

"*No. Why, Max?*"

"*WHY NOT?!*"

"Because she has these special . . . uh . . . these monster-proof . . . uh . . . shoes."

"*SHOES? DID YOU SAY THE WORD OF 'SHOES'?!*" Pip squeaked. "*WHAT ARE YOU SAYING TO US, MAX?!*"

"Yeah. Shoes." Max looked at me again.

"Monster-proof shoes," I repeated. Max was weaving a very tangly web tonight.

"*THE SOPHIE HAS SPECIAL NO-MONSTER SHOES? WHERE ARE THOSE THINGS THE SIZE OF GUINEA PIG FEET FOR TEDDY AND ME?!*"

"You guys don't need 'em 'cuz you have the towels. Monsters stay away from the shoes just as much as the towels. Like, the same amount."

"*That is true, Pip. We are not needing the shoes if we have chicken towels. Everyone knows that thing, even you. But surely we should have let the Sophie take a towel for her time out of this safe kitchen. And Amelia, too! Oops!*"

"Actually, I'm pretty sure I saw Amelia, like, grab one of those on the way out," Max said quickly. "And Sophie only needs the shoes, like I said. And, also, did you know that monsters don't like rain?"

Lightning. Thunder. BOOM! BOOM!!

"*Monsters do not like the wet, wet, wet rainy-rain? Monsters are afraid of the booming booms?*"

"Yep. It's true. If they get wet, they . . . uh . . . they melt. So they all took off, right out of Westerfield. Like, far away. Maybe to another state. Maybe to New Hampshire." Max grinned at me.

Teddy looked up at him. "*Rain makes monsters melt? Like the scary, green-faced witches from the place of Oz, Max? Is this the truly-truth, or are you making up stories or jokes?*"

"*MOLLY JANE, IS MAX PLAYING TRICKS?!*"

Instead of answering, I said, "I'm sorry Sophie has to be out in the storm. I mean, it's because of me."

"What? No it isn't, Mol. Of course it isn't."

"It is too! She wanted to help me even more then she already did."

"Aw, don't be sorry, Molly. That's just how she is," Max said. "She is so awesome that way, like, way too good for a guy like me," he mumbled.

"What? That is not true."

"*YES, IT IS TOO TRUE! TEE HEE!*"

"She likes you," I said. "I can tell."

Max's eyes flickered to me. "Yeah? For real? You can tell?"

"*Excuse me, Max,*" Teddy said, "*we already told you and told you this same stuff, time and again. It is not the time for talking about if the Sophie is liking of sloppy Max or not liking. There are monsters out there! That is the situation!*"

"Yeah, well, don't you little dudes worry about a thing. I have it all under control."

"*MAX, YOU CANNOT HAVE THE CONTROL OF MONSTERS.*"

Max turned his attention to me. "Mol? Go ahead and do another run-through of the presentation, huh? Let's get our minds off of the storm and, uh, other things . . ."

"*Things like tapping, clicking monsters?*"

". . . and back onto New Hampshire."

"*LET US NOT! NEW HAMPSHIRE STINKS!*"

"Pipster, dude, what's with the attitude?"

"New Hampshire is great," I said. "Help me win a ribbon tomorrow, okay?"

"*OKAY, MOLLY JANE. NEW HAMPSHIRE ONLY STINKS A LITTLE BIT. TEE HEE!*"

"Sorry, Molly Jane. When Pip is feeling the stress, he says a lot of things about 'stink,'" Teddy said.

"Anyway," I said louder than the noisy weather, "the largest of New Hampshire's lakes is Lake Winnipesaukee." There was a crack of thunder, then the sound of rain hitting the windows.

"*A NO-GOOD LAKE FULL OF MELTED-UP MONSTERS, RIGHT MAX?*" Pip giggled.

"Right," Max chuckled, then he looked at me and said, "Sorry, Mol. Go on."

"Captain John Mason named this land 'New Hampshire' after the English county of Hampshire," I went on. The rain was really loud now.

"*HE NAMED IT A NO-GOOD NAME!*" Pip giggled. "*IT SHOULD INSTEAD HAVE THE NAME OF 'NEW MELTED MONSTER'!*"

"Granite is the state rock of New Hampshire —"

"*GRANITE IS A ROCK THAT IS . . . NO GOOD! TEE HEE!*"

"*Tee hee!*"

"Come on, you sillies," I said. "Stop being so goofy. I need to practice."

"*Silly and goofy is what we are being! Look at us being those things!*"

"*GOOFY-GOOF-GOOF! SILLY-SILL-SILL!*"

"Well, at least you know that this is the hardest it'll be, as far as doing your presentation. Right? 'Cuz tomorrow, you won't have a storm or furry little hecklers in the crowd."

"But I'll have fifth-grade boys, and especially Benny Nubb."

"*NUBB, BLUB, NUBB, BLUB, NUBB!*"

"Okay. Where was I? You guys are making me cuckoo!" I said. "Oh yeah, the state symbols. The capital city of New Hampshire is Concord. The state motto is 'Live free or die'. And here are some of the symbols of New Hampshire: the state bird is the purple finch, animal is the white-tailed deer, insect – the ladybug. The state fruit is the pumpkin, flower – purple lilac, tree – white birch, and the state sport is skiing."

"*SKIING SOUNDS SILLY! NEW HAMPSHIRE SOUNDS NO GOOD, AND ALSO SILLY! THE STATE BIRD IS SILLY!*"

"Okay, crazy Pip, that is enough 'stink,' and also 'silly.' It is now time to say something is good about Molly Jane's state, or else be very quiet."

"*OBJECTION!*"

"*I dare you, crazy Pip! I think you cannot do those things – be quiet or say something good about*

Molly Jane's state. That is the dare in this situation. I think you will not do it. That is what I think. So I win."

"Dude, Teddy just threw down the gauntlet," Max laughed. "What're you gonna do?"

"*OBJECTION! TEDDY NEEDS TO STOP THROWING THINGS AT PIP OR I WILL THROW MAIL BACK AT HIM!*"

"*Be quiet or say something good about Molly Jane's state,*" Teddy said again. "*That is what I am throwing at you, crazy Pip.*"

Pip gave Teddy a long long look, shook his head, fired him, then started to sing.

New Hampshire is good
Live there we all should
Houses made of wood
New Hampshire is good!

Finch birds in trees
Lilacs in the breeze
Live live free!
New Hampshire is good!

Pumpkins, lady bugs
Ski and ski and ski
Live live free!
New Hampshire is good!

Granite is the thing
Deers are frolicking
Guinea pigs are king!
New Hampshire is good!

Everyone stared when the song was finished, and then Pip said, "*TA-DA! TEE HEE! I WIN THE DARE AND SAVE THE DAY!*"

"Pipster! That was awesome! You are the man!" Max laughed. "You did that, like, right on the spot?"

"*YES, MAX, PIP IS THE MAN! PIP IS THE DUDE! PIP IS ON THE SPOT!*"

"I love it, Pip," I said.

"*Good job on writing a song about good,*" Teddy said. "*Now how about the one about being quiet? That is the new dare.*"

"Do you think you could sing that again, like, in front of a microphone?" Max looked excited and like wheels were turning in his head.

"*DUDE, I AM A ROCK STAR. OF COURSE I CAN DO THAT THING! WHERE IS THE IDOL MICROPHONE?*"

"And Teddy, buddy? Could you stand next to Pip while he's singing and, you know, be the back-up singer? Do some grooving?"

"*Max, what is this grooving you are talking about? It sounds silly.*"

"Move your head from side to side — like, look real cool-like?" Max demonstrated and the guinea pigs both giggled.

"*Max, you silly, why do you want me to do that thing? It is time now for Pip to stop screaming and singing. Right, Max? Right? Say I am right, please.*"

"Buddy, trust me on this. I have an idea, and it'll be totally awesome."

"*I will think about it, but possibly and probably I will say 'no' about this one, Max,*" Teddy said. "*Ideas about Pip making more noise are not my favorite kind.*"

"Okay, you think on it, buddy. Let me know when you decide. Mol? Let's take it from the top!"

But suddenly, all of the lights went out.

The storm stopped and all was quiet inside and out.

TAP TAP TAP . . . TAP TAP TAP!
TAP TAP TAP . . . TAP TAP TAP!

All except for that.

Chapter Seventeen
In the dark

Did that scare you? Are you okay?

Lucky for us, Max turned on his phone flashlight right away. It was very bright and flashy, so we could see a little bit. "Let's see if we can find something to brighten things up," he said. He started to open and close drawers and cabinets until he found some candles. "How about these?"

Before too long, the kitchen was lit up with glowing candlelight. But also shadows on the walls that made Teddy and Pip very nervous — so nervous that they wanted to go back to the igloo and be covered with towels.

TAP TAP TAP . . . TAP TAP TAP!
TAP TAP TAP . . . TAP TAP TAP!

And there was still that.

"*GO AWAY, GHOSTS AND MONSTERS! WALLY IS NOT IN THIS HOUSE! GO FIND HIM IN THE NEW HAMPSHIRE LAKE! GO, GO, GO! YOU WON'T MELT! GO TRY IT!*"

"*Molly Jane! Surely it is time now for us all to go to your house, right?!*"

"Max?" I called with a shaky voice. He had left the kitchen to go to the dark, scary basement with his phone a long time ago. He was looking for the fuse box so he could do whatever a person did with those things. "Max?"

TAP TAP TAP . . . TAP TAP TAP!
TAP TAP TAP . . . TAP TAP TAP!

I swallowed hard. It was dumb to be nervous. The tapping was done by Benny Nubb, not . . . not anything else. Definitely not by monsters.

Benny Nubb. That boy was unbelievable! The second it stopped pouring down rain, there he was, tapping on the window!

TAP TAP TAP . . . TAP TAP TAP!
TAP TAP TAP . . . TAP TAP TAP!

Where in the world was Mrs. Nubb? Why was it so hard to keep her kid under control?

"Guys, if you will let me go to the living room for two seconds and look out the window, I can . . ."

"NO, NO, NO! MOLLY JANE MUST STAY WITH US!"

". . . catch him red-handed . . ."

"NO!"

". . . and close the case once and for all!"

"*Please do not go out to the darkly dark room where monsters are tapping and peeking in! Please, Molly Jane!*"

"STAY, STAY, STAY! PUT A CHICKEN TOWEL ON YOUR HEAD LIKE US, MOLLY JANE! MONSTERS DON'T LIKE THOSE THINGS! DO NOT GO! NO NO!"

"Okay," I sighed. "Okay, guys, calm down. I'm staying."

"*Good job, Molly Jane!*"

"*CHICKEN TOWEL, MOLLY JANE! LET ME SEE YOU DO THAT THING — PUT IT ON YOUR HEAD! MOLLY JANE? MOLLY JANE? WHY ARE YOU NOT DOING WHAT I SAY TO DO?*"

"Max?" I called.

Nothing. Except. . . .

TAP TAP TAP . . . TAP TAP TAP!

"Max?" I called again. "Um, Max?"

"*MONSTERS GOT OUR MAX!*"

"*Is it true, Molly Jane? Did those clickety monsters crunch up that dude? Oh no!*"

"No. Of course not," I said, but my voice was really thin when I called again. "Mmmmax?"

"I'm right here, guys," Max appeared in the kitchen and made all of us jump. "I think the whole street lost power," he said, peeking out the window.

"*DO NOT MOVE THE TOWEL!*" Pip squeaked at him.

"Sorry." Max moved away from the window with his hands up.

"Oh no! Poor Tweets!" I said. "Max! He's at my house alone in the dark!"

TAP TAP TAP . . . TAP TAP TAP!

"Mol, I'm sure Mr. Feathers is fine for a little while in the dark. I mean, birds don't mind darkness. I don't think. He's fine. I'm sure."

"How can you be sure about something like that?"

TAP TAP TAP . . . TAP TAP TAP!
TAP TAP TAP . . . TAP TAP TAP!

I waved Max close to me, and, real quiet so Teddy and Pip wouldn't hear, whispered right in his ear, "Will you look out the window by the front door? I'd do it, but they don't want me to leave."

Max nodded.

"Wait until you hear the taps again. Benny Nubb is out there. I know it." I took a deep breath. "Solve the mystery, okay? Do it for all of us."

Keeping his phone flashlight beaming in front of him, Max headed for the living room.

Chapter Eighteen
Amelia's front door

"Nobody out there!" Max called.

"What? Impossible!" I called back. "Look harder!"

"*MAX CANNOT SEE INVISIBLE MONSTERS, MOLLY JANE! HE DOES NOT HAVE THE RIGHT EYES FOR THAT. MOLLY JANE, TELL MAX THAT THING, OR ELSE THEY ARE GOING TO CRUNCH HIM ALL UP!*"

"You guys, it's Benny Nubb," I said, straining my ears to hear Max.

"Nothing!" he called again.

"But how can that *be*?!"

Tap tap tap tap tap!

I jumped because Max was right behind me all of a sudden.

Tap tap tap tap tap!!

"There it is again," I whispered, "only different." The noise was softer, less steady. How come? What did it mean? "How can he tap like that and get away so fast?"

Tap tap tap tap tap! Tap. Tap?!

"*Girl monsters,*" Teddy whispered. "*That is girl-monster clicking.*"

"GIRL MONSTERS ARE STILL NO-GOOD MONSTERS!"

"I'll go check again," Max said with a shrug.

The kitchen was very quiet while we waited.

Max said, "This time there's someone out there."

I couldn't believe it when I heard him open the door right on up.

For Sophie.

While Sophie was around, Teddy and Pip could not talk about monsters, so that was a relief to my nerves. Plus, she was not scared one little bit, and that helped all of us to calm down a few notches.

But still, in-between the work we were doing and Sophie's happy talking or humming, there it was, again and again:

TAP TAP TAP . . . TAP TAP TAP!

What . . . ? How . . . ? I tried and tried to figure out how he was doing it, but my brain would not budge. How could he do those taps and then run away so fast that Max couldn't see him?

"These headbands are adorable," Sophie said, pulling my brain back to my State Fair project. She held one up to the candlelight, then put it on her head. "And our pictures are going to be amazing. And Max's idea. . . ." She put two fingers over her mouth. "Whoops! I wasn't supposed to mention that yet. Never mind."

Max had been doing secret things out in the dark living room, but popped into the kitchen when he heard his name. He held out a hand, and – huh? Sophie handed him a headband. Which was totally cuckoo.

I actually felt some relief when he didn't put it on his head.

It got quiet while Max stood there, smiling a dopey smile at Sophie, holding that headband.

TAP TAP TAP . . . TAP TAP TAP!

"What is that?" Sophie finally noticed the tapping. "That tapping noise. Do you guys hear that, too?"

"Max?" I gave him a secret look as Teddy and Pip started some noisy whooping and wheeking. "Would you go check, please?"

"I swear, there was nothing out there, and I've already checked ten times." Max saw my eyebrows going up and up. "But I'll go look again. Be right back," he added, then smiled at Sophie some more. He left the room backwards and bumped into the doorway. "Ow."

"Teddy and Pip? Are you two sweeties afraid of that tapping sound?" Sophie left her chair and headed for the walkway. She pulled the safe, magical purple igloo right off of them, chicken towels and all.

But I guess she has a magical touch with guinea pigs, too, because when she lifted Teddy up and cuddled him, he got quiet. "It's okay, sweetie," she said. "I'm here. Sophie is here. You're okay. It's only a funny little noise."

TAP TAP TAP . . . TAP TAP TAP!

Of course, Pip went crazy-jealous and started wheeking louder than ever before in the history of Pip.

TAP TAP TAP . . . TAP TAP TAP!

I picked him up and wrapped him in a towel. "All *safe* and snug in your chicken towel," I said.

TAP TAP TAP . . . TAP. . . .

Ding dong!

Huh?

"I wonder who that could be," Sophie said.

"Yeah. . . ." I frowned. "I'm going to peek around the corner and see," I said. "It's a person," I added for Pip's sake because now he was wheeking like a fire engine siren. "Only people ring doorbells. Pip, shh! Okay? Please?"

He quieted way down, but I could feel his little body trembling. When we got close to the dark living room he whispered, "*NO, NO, NO!*" Then his head disappeared under the towel.

I really would've rather seen a monster than what I did see in Amelia's doorway. "It's Benny Nubb," I whispered to Pip.

"*LET ME SEE! I WANT TO SEE THAT NUBB!*"

"Why? No, let's go back to the kitchen," I said, and ducked around the corner with a scrunched-up face. "I can't believe it!"

"*I, TOO, CAN'T BELIEVE IT!*" Pip squeaked in a smallish voice.

"Well, maybe now you and Teddy will believe me about who is doing the taps. Now that that boy is in this house, there won't be any tapping."

"*MAYBE. BUT ALSO I WANT TO SEE WHAT A NUBB IS ALL ABOUT, MOLLY JANE! LET ME SEE!*"

"Okay, okay, but only if you shh!"

"*ALWAYS TONIGHT YOU ARE SAYING 'SHHH' TO ME, MOLLY JANE! STOP THAT!*"

"Sorry," I whispered, as we crept back into the living room.

Mrs. Nubb was standing behind her kid, holding a big, bright lantern, like the kind you use for camping. Benny Nubb was staring down at the floor. His mom gave him a little push, but he still didn't look up.

"Amelia and Wally aren't home right now," Max said in a polite way, like he had forgotten all about earlier and how he had needed to grab and wrestle with Benny Nubb in my front yard. "I can have Amelia call you when she's back, which should be in about an hour, I suppose."

"That will be fine," Mrs. Nubb said. "Benny will be at the Fisher's for a while, anyway. He can stop by after he's finished there."

I scrunched up my face about that.

"*THERE IS A MOM-NUBB HERE IN OUR HOUSE, TOO!?*" Pip whispered. "*NUBB AND NUBB, MOLLY JANE!*"

"Actually, Molly's here with me," Max said.

"She is? Oh, is that Molly right there?" Pip disappeared under the towel as Mrs. Nubb shined her lantern right on my face. "Well. Benjamin? Change of plans. You're staying right here. You know what you need to do, son." She set the lantern down on the guinea pigs' walkway and crossed her arms. When her kid didn't do anything, she gave him a push.

He only looked up enough so he wouldn't trip or run into anything. When he was close enough to me, he looked back down at his hands instead of at my face. "Sorry about the map," he mumbled. Then he shoved something at me and zoomed back by his mom.

It was a ten dollar bill. I am not even kidding about that. I stared at it.

"Benjamin? What in the name of Pete are you . . . ?" Mrs. Nubb rushed over and plucked the money right back out of my hand. "Benny is here to offer his *help* to you tonight, Molly. Use him in any way you see fit." She shook her head a lot, then turned to go. "I am certain that later this evening Molly will tell me how helpful and courteous you were tonight," she said to her not-helpful, not-courteous, bribing kid. Then she took the big lantern and left in a rush.

Except for the glowing red bird decoration behind the curtains, the living room got totally dark after Mrs. Nubb left. Plus awkward and quiet. Benny Nubb didn't say a thing, just stood there.

Max said, "Uh. . . ." Then he said, "Well, look, uh. . . ."

Nubb shoved his hands into his pockets and mumbled a sentence under his breath that had the word "dumb" in it.

"*NO GOOD!*" Pip whispered.

I cuddled Pip very close to me so Benny Nubb would not see him and do or say something mean.

Max clapped his hands together and said, "Why don't we head for the kitchen where there's some light, and then you can meet Sophie?" Too bad for him, he had to be the grown-up in the situation.

I left the room in a hurry. Holy moly. My luck was up and down so much and so fast today that I was getting seasick from it. Was Mrs. Nubb cuckoo? Did she really think it was going to be helpful for real to make her grumpy kid hang around here tonight, when I had so much to do? Really?

"Benny, this is Sophie," Max said. "Sophie . . . uh . . . Benny, the neighbor."

Sophie looked up from her work and smiled.

I was glad she didn't gush or say something too nice. I might have had to throw up about that.

"He's here to help Mol with her project," Max said, without explaining it any more than that.

"Well, we sure have lots for you to help with, Benny!" she said.

He mumbled, "Whatever."

"No we don't," I muttered, then turned away from that boy. His beady eyes were trying to figure out what was growling at him from under the chicken towels.

"Let's see . . . he could help decorate the special cookies for your grandmas, Molly. Benny, how do you feel about decorating cookies?" Sophie asked.

He did a big shrug and said, "Dunno."

"I'm going to do that," I said. "I want them to be really special."

I saw that boy's eyes narrow up at me and thought maybe that was a mean-sounding thing to say. I felt a little bit bad.

Sophie tried again. "How about addressing the envelopes? Molly is making a special card for each of her grandmas at Shady Acres, and they all need to go in special envelopes. Do you . . . ?"

"I want to do those, too," I said, stepping in front of the pile on the table. "I'm doing the names in purple glitter glue, and —"

"Okay . . . ?" Sophie looked at Max for help.

"Molly needs to practice her presentation for the State Fair," Max said. "How about if you be the audience with me? All you have to do is sit and listen."

"No!" I said, moving in front of the project board. "He can't. He's a kid judge tomorrow, so he can't see it early. It wouldn't be fair."

Benny Nubb scowled at me and crossed his arms real tight. "Whatever," he mumbled.

"Mol, we have to find something for him to do," Max quietly tried to reason with me.

"Benny, how are you with a camera?" Sophie said, brightening up her smile.

"I dunno. Why?"

"Well, we are going to —"

I started to argue and not let him help with that, either, and that's when Teddy and Pip decided not to be quiet anymore. At the same time, even though Teddy was in the igloo and Pip was being held by me, and was under towels, they started wheeking and doing sirens — some of their loudest ever.

"*EEEEEOOOOOEEEEEOOOOO!*"

"*Wheek! Wheek! Wheek! Wheek! Wheek! Wheek!*"

"*EEEEEOOOOOEEEEEOOOOO!*"

"*Wheek! Wheek! Wheek! Wheek! Wheek! Wheek!*"

Nobody expected that noisy thing. I don't know what they were trying to accomplish, but it did break up the thick-as-pea-soup tension in that room. Sophie giggled and put her hand over her mouth. Max was so surprised, he backed up into a chair and almost knocked it over.

And Benny Nubb uncrossed his arms and opened his eyes up real wide. "Are those guinea pigs?" he asked.

"EEEEEOOOOOEEEEOOOOO!"

"*Wheek! Wheek! Wheek! Wheek! Wheek! Wheek!*"

"EEEEEEEEEEEEEEEEEEEEEEEEEEEEE EOOOOOOOOOOOOOOOO!"

"*Wheeeeeeek!*"

"Yes indeed," Sophie giggled. "That is Teddy," she said, pointing to the cute face peeking out of the igloo, "and Molly is holding Pip."

"Where is he? What's he wrapped up for?" Benny Nubb was Sir Talks-a-lot now. He pointed at the chicken towel. "And why's he making that loud sound?"

"Because he's scared," I said. "They both are, and the towels make them feel better."

"What're they scared of?"

I closed my mouth tight and made my eyes little slits. It was very hard not to do sarcasm at him.

"They didn't like the storm, or those tapping noises," Max said, sharing a look with me.

"What tapping noises?" Benny Nubb wanted to know.

"At least there won't be any of those while you're in here," I said, then walked away from him.

"Hey! What does that mean?"

"Nothing," I mumbled.

"I didn't do anything," he said in a loud voice. "Why do you keep saying stuff like that? My mom was making me apologize to these neighbors for stuff I didn't even do tonight! And that is no fair! What's the deal, anyway?"

"Mol, why don't we think of something that Benny can help with?" Max begged, as the tension got to be pea soup again. "There must be something."

I shrugged. My face felt red as a tomato. Teddy's whoops were steady and loud, and Pip was kind of hurting my ears.

"We were just about to start taking pictures of the guinea pigs!" Sophie said over all of it, trying to rescue everyone and brighten up the gloomy, soupy scene. "Do you want to be our photographer?"

"I dunno," Benny said again. "Maybe." He was back to mumbly and muttering, but he looked a little bit interested, too.

"Molly? Do you think these two will agree to put on the hats I made them?" Sophie asked.

I took a deep breath, let it out, and focused. Never mind about Benny Nubb. I had a project to finish, a ribbon to win, and no time to waste. "They wore Christmas hats for me. And also wedding hats."

Sophie smiled. "Oh yeah?"

"I have pictures, I'll show you later. So, yeah. I think so," I said. "What kind of hats?"

"New Hampshire stuff. Want to see?"

Benny Nubb said, "New Hampshire?"

I ignored him and looked at Sophie's adorable little guinea pig hats.

"Did you say New Hampshire?" he asked again.

"Molly's state for the fair is New Hampshire," Max said.

"That's the one I did last year."

I actually turned to look at him, shocked, because that was a humongous coincidence — if he wasn't lying.

When we were facing that boy, Pip peeked out of the chicken towel and did some quieter whoops.

Then maybe, just maybe, I saw that boy's face turn into . . . not a smile, but not a not-smile. "Hey," he said, "there he is. And he's looking at me."

"*WORST OF TIMES,*" Pip whispered. "*WhooooOOP!*"

"What was his name? Pip?"

"It's a great name," I said. "The best, except for Teddy. It's a tie."

"I didn't say it wasn't great." Benny Nubb's voice was grouchy again. "I only asked."

"Anyway," Sophie interrupted, "where should we take the pictures? Let's get started. This will be lots of fun!"

I didn't know about that. If he wasn't there, maybe, but. . . .

"You don't have enough light," Benny Nubb said.

"Oh my gosh, you're right," Sophie giggled. "That is a bit of a problem. Max? Any ideas?"

Max peeked out the window, which made Teddy and Pip go cuckoo all over again. "Power's still out, far as I can see. Guess we'll have to wait. But in the meantime —"

"We'll have to do it in here," I said. "The guys are afraid to leave the kitchen."

"How come?" Benny Nubb wanted to know.

As if he wasn't the reason. I did not give him an answer.

"They sure are in a state tonight," Sophie said, then laughed. "A state, get it? I didn't even mean to say that!"

"We need something solid for a background, or to put on the table," Max said, looking around the kitchen, "like...."

"I have a flag."

Gee whiz, now that boy wanted to put his two cents in everywhere! I looked at him. "What flag? What do you mean?"

"New Hampshire."

"You do not have a New Hampshire flag," I said.

"Do too."

"Do not."

He crossed his arms real tight. "Do. Too. I got it for my project last year. Do you want to use it, or not?"

"Oh, cool!" Sophie said. "Isn't that cool, Molly?"

"Maybe." That was all I could manage to say. "If you really have one."

"I do. So . . . you're gonna put hats on these guinea pigs and take their pictures? And then what? What's that got to do with New Hampshire?"

I turned toward him to tell him that it was a secret, and Pip decided to peek out of the towel. He looked at Benny just as hard as that boy was looking at him. His little nose was twitching like crazy, but he was quiet.

"He's cute."

Whoa. Wait a second, did those two words really come out of that mean mouth? "I thought you hated guinea pigs."

He frowned hard and said, "No."

Pip said a short and loud, "*WHEEE!*" It was something new for him and sounded really funny. He did it again. "*WHEEE!*"

Even though I didn't want to, I smiled. "Pip? What are you saying?"

Benny Nubb got surprised by it and backed up, almost smiling again. He looked at Pip and said, "Oh yeah? You think so, huh?"

"*WHEEE!*"

Benny Nubb did another almost-smile and did more staring with Pip. Then he wandered over to Teddy, who was out of the igloo and standing up on his back paws, looking. "Are you gonna yell at me, too? Might as well get it over with. Hit me with it."

Teddy looked and looked at that boy, long and hard. Then he did a very un-Teddy-ish thing and copied Pip. "*WHEEE!*"

That time, Benny Nubb actually did smile. For three whole seconds. "These guys are funny," he said. "I mean, they're like little people. Sorta."

"They're awesome," I said back.

"Hey, I know!" He looked like a light bulb was going off in his head. He said it to Sophie, his biggest fan in the room, then said, "I'll be right back," and ran out of the house.

Chapter Nineteen
What is up with that Nubb?

The laughs and other excited sounds from the living room told me that Max and Sophie's secret meeting was something I totally wanted to overhear. But I stayed in the kitchen and did not wreck Max's surprise. And I had a talk with Teddy and Pip.

"What were you two up to with Benny Nubb? It seemed like you were being nice, and that doesn't make sense."

"*WE WERE NOT UP TO THINGS! WE ARE NICE GUYS!*"

"Right. Try again," I said, shaking my head.

"*Molly Jane, it is not a big secret what we were 'up to,' as you say it. Pip and me like to do a thing called 'give a person a chance.'*"

"What? Since when?" I laughed.

"*We never saw that Nubb before this day we are in. We only heard of him from you and Amelia about maybe his mischief. So we needed to give that Nubb a look-see before our deciding about good or no good. That is how we roll, Pip and me.*"

"*THAT'S HOW WE ROLL, MOLLY JANE!*"

"That's how you . . . ? Now, wait just a minute," I said, putting my hands on my hips. "That is not how you roll. What about my mom? What about Max?"

"*MOM JANE PUT US IN A BUCKET!*" Pip said, getting right in my face. "*BUT MAX IS A DUDE!*"

"And you totally decided that he was no good before you ever saw him," I reminded them. "You were upset that he was coming to stay with you, not wanting to give him a chance of any kind, and then you tried to get him to leave all weekend."

"*That is not the point of the point here, Molly Jane!*" Teddy said.

"Isn't it?"

"*NO! THE POINT IS A NUBB AND MONSTERS ARE CLICKING, SO DO NOT ARGUE WITH US, MOLLY JANE!*"

"Huh?"

"*The point here is that we guinea pigs give chances before we decide on good or no good. Sometimes. Or most of the time. Except probably for that Max. Sometimes we break our own rules, Molly Jane. Guinea pigs can do that thing.*"

"*WE CAN! WE CAN ROLL LIKE THAT, OR SOME OTHER WAY IF WE WANT!*"

"*Anyways or anyhow, we needed to check out the Nubb most closely to surely know that he is not doing tapping mischief outside our haunted house like Molly Jane and Amelia say and say to us. Now we are sure. Nubb has stub fingers, just like we guessed. Not clickety ones.*" Teddy scratched his ear. "*The carrot-ory, Molly Jane, is that there are monsters out there. Now it is for sure, and we need to fix that problem. The problem is not about Nubb.*"

"What's a carrot-ory? You guys never told me what that means."

"*NUBB, GLUB, BLUB! NOT IN THE CLUB! TEE HEE! BUT HE IS NOT A MONSTER, MOLLY JANE, AND THAT MEANS FOR SURE THE MONSTERS ARE TAPPING, AND THEY ARE NOT GOING AWAY!*" Pip looked right at me, his little face very close to mine, until I had to smile. Then he started sniffing at Sophie's little hats, which were lined up on the walkway.

"*Nubb is not a cheery boy with laughs and smiles, that is for sure,*" Teddy said quietly. "*But I am thinking that that does not mean he is all no-good. Wait and see what he does, Molly Jane. It is the doing, not the grumpy face, that matters. So far, this day, he is not doing bad stuff. Only grumping. That is what Pip is like most of the time, and he is not all bad.*"

"*OBJECTION!*"

"He broke my map all to pieces, Teddy," I said.

"*DO NOT SPEAK OF MAPS!*"

"*And I am sad for you about that, Molly Jane. Very. But he said the word of 'sorry.' And that means . . . sorry.*"

"I don't think he meant it."

"*We can't be sure, but we will see,*" Teddy said. "*Right, Molly Jane? Best friend who gives chances to people and also others, even Pip?*"

"I didn't give Sophie a chance."

"*WHAT ARE YOU SAYING, MOLLY JANE?! WHY NOT?!*"

"*Why would you not think that the Sophie is good?*" Teddy wanted to know. "*I love the Sophie!*"

"*I, TOO, LOVE THE SOPHIE!*"

"I don't know, exactly. But now I know she's great and a real friend."

"*Yes, Molly Jane, that is the truth of it.*"

"*THE SOPHIE IS GOOD!*"

"The thing is, if I had given her a chance in the first place — had stayed put and gotten to know her like Max wanted me to, instead of going to Nora's right away — the map wouldn't have broken —"

"*YOU TALKED AGAIN OF MAPS, MOLLY JANE! STOP THAT!*"

"Max would've given me a ride to Nora's house if it was raining hard, so Benny Nubb wouldn't have made me drop the box. And then he would not be bugging us tonight. Well, except for. . . ." I stopped and listened. No tapping, for the moment.

But some good stuff happened after the bad stuff, and my project was cooler than ever.

It was actually a whole lot to think about, those "what-ifs," and the more I thought about it, the more cuckoo I got.

TAP TAP TAP . . . TAP TAP TAP!
TAP TAP TAP . . . TAP TAP TAP!

Unbelievable. And I had almost given that boy another chance.

"*Monsters, Molly Jane!*" Teddy squeaked. "*For surely monsters! Go away, monsters!*"

"*MONSTERS! MONSTERS! MONSTERS!*"

Teddy and Pip disappeared into the purple igloo just as lights popped on all over the house.

Ding dong.

Ugh. Somehow I knew that the doorbell dinging meant Benny Nubb was back.

Sophie rushed to the door, but I stayed in the kitchen with Teddy and Pip. I could hear her talking out there, and she was excited. Like, really excited.

Well, whatever. Never mind that mean boy and his mischief or his flag. I had projects to finish. Now that I had light, I could finish writing my grandmas' names on those envelopes. The finished ones were spread out on Amelia's counter, glitter glue drying, in alphabetical order by first name, next to the plate of cookies with names on them. But I didn't even get one started before they all walked in.

"Molly, look!" Sophie's eyes were shiny, her smile humongous.

I didn't want to look, because whatever it was, it was about that mean boy. But I had to. I slowly turned around.

Benny Nubb was holding a small pink carrying case. Pink. And the pink carrying case was . . . huh? Whooping?

Whoop whoop whoop whoop!

Huh? What? I tried hard not to be interested, but holy moly was I ever interested! "What is that?"

"It's a guinea pig! Oh, Molly!" Sophie gushed. "Look at her!"

Her? That boy had a girl guinea pig and carried her around in a pink case? He set the case down on the table, and I peeked in. Through the slats, I could see a guinea pig nose, sniffing like crazy. "Oh my gosh," I breathed, because she was so cute. "Hi there," I said. "What's your name?"

"Her name is Linny."

I turned my eyes away from the little girl guinea pig and stared at the boy who was making no sense all of a sudden.

His face got pink enough to match the case. "She's my cousin's. I'm watching her."

"You have a girl cousin who you're *helping*?"

He frowned at me.

"I mean, that's nice of you."

"If you want, you can pick her up." He popped open the case. "She likes people."

Linny looked right up at me and maybe she nodded her head to agree about that.

"It's okay, I don't . . ." I argued even though I really wanted to pick her up.

She stood up with her paws against the carrier, like she wanted me to pick her up, and oh my gosh, she was very cute and friendly.

"You can pick her up," he said again. "She likes it."

I picked her up. She was very soft, small, and sweet, and I felt her rough little tongue on my knuckles. "Hi," I said again, and part of my brain expected her to say "hi" back. Out of the corner of my eye, I saw Teddy and Pip peeking out of their igloo. They were being quiet, probably totally jealous. I waited for them to start up a ruckus, but they didn't. Maybe they were giving the little guinea pig a chance, because sometimes they did that.

"I brought the flag. And this is a lizard. I mean, a newt – the state whatever. It's a rubber one. You can borrow it. If you want. My project wasn't very good, but I have this stuff. And maybe Linny could help with the hats. Or whatever. So . . ." Benny Nubb shrugged.

He moved the pink case off of the table, set the flag on it, then set down the newt. He moved it a bit this way, then that, then nodded with satisfaction.

Sophie and Max were totally spying on us from the doorway, so I said, "Thank you."

"It's a spotted newt," he said, poking the orange, rubbery thing. "Cool, huh?"

"Cool," I said, even though I am not a fan of reptiles of any kind. "Thank you," I said again. Then I held Linny up to my cheek.

"*Wheek wheek!*"

"She's a good guinea pig," Benny Nubb said. "Those guys are good, too. I mean, they're cool." He pointed to Teddy and Pip, who were keeping quiet so far.

"Teddy and Pip are the best," I said, but didn't say it in a grumpy way, actually. My mood was getting better for some reason, probably because of the soft, sweet guinea pig in my hands. "If you want, you could. . . ." Huh? I had almost offered to let him hold one of them.

Teddy, that amazing little guy, must've read my mind somehow. He left the igloo and started whooping. Then he stood up against the ledge, like, totally inviting someone to pick him up. Which he never does.

"You could hold Teddy," I said slowly. "But. . . ." Then I stopped myself from being bossy at him. "If you want," I said instead.

Benny Nubb scooped Teddy right up, then held him — in the right way. "Hi," he said to Teddy.

And Teddy said a single, "*Whoop!*"

Pip turned into a fire engine siren.

"What is all this?" Benny Nubb asked as he started following the walkway out of the kitchen. "What's this, Teddy? I've never seen a thing like this before."

"It's a guinea pig walkway," I said. "Wally made this so they can walk all over the house whenever they want," I said, following him.

"Cool," he said. He stopped at the house and said, "Whoa," then looked inside. "Did he make this, too? I've never seen a guinea pig house like this before."

"Yes," I said. "Your neighbor Wally is an amazing builder. And also a college professor. Did you know that?"

"Nah, I didn't know that," he mumbled. "Cool. And is that your TV, Teddy? You guys have a lot of cool stuff." He did some more walking. "This walkway thing goes all around and around. Cool." He stopped by the front windows and pulled back the curtain.

I could feel Teddy getting scared and nervous, totally afraid of the living room and the window. He started up some steady wheeking and snorting.

"It's okay, boy," Benny said. "I've got ya. You're okay." He poked a finger at the glowing bird decoration thing, said "cool" again, then let the curtain fall back over the window.

Teddy calmed down, and I followed them back to the kitchen. Sophie was taking care of noisy, jealous Pip. "You're watching a guinea pig," I said, still shocked about that, "but you have a big dog."

"Aw, Rufus don't hurt nothing. He gets into these guys' yard sometimes. But he don't mean anything by it. He wouldn't hurt another animal. Or a person. No way."

"But you said he'd eat Nora's guinea pig."

He looked at me with a frown on his face. "No I didn't. Or if I did, I didn't mean it."

"Then why'd you say it?"

"I don't know." He shrugged. "It was dumb. I didn't mean it."

For some reason, I believed him about that and let it drop.

He nodded at Linny. "She likes to eat lettuce, like, a lot. Do they have any of that here?"

"Of course they do. These guys like it too. Like, they totally love it."

Teddy started wheeking at the word "lettuce." Pip, who had just quieted down, joined in. It got pretty noisy, and the noise made Sophie giggle.

"Whoa. All I did was talk about it, and they're all excited," Benny Nubb said. "It's like they know what the word means. She gets noisy soon as I open the fridge." He nodded his head at Linny. "So get ready."

I opened the refrigerator door and — he was right — she started wheeking. She knew what an opened refrigerator could mean.

Benny Nubb reached around me and said, "Aha!" then grabbed two ready-to-go crinkly plastic bags.

And all three guinea pigs went nuts. The kitchen was completely cuckoo. And I mean *totally* noisy with guinea pig wheeking. Max started laughing because Sophie was laughing, and — holy moly —

Benny Nubb was even laughing. It was a total miracle caused by guinea pig cuteness.

And then....

TAP TAP TAP... TAP TAP TAP!
TAP TAP TAP... TAP TAP TAP!

Every single one of us, humans and guinea pigs, got quiet. (Well, the guinea pigs were only quiet because they were munching away at their veggies.)

TAP TAP TAP... TAP TAP TAP!
TAP TAP TAP... TAP TAP TAP!
TAP TAP TAP... TAP TAP TAP!

I turned slowly to look at Max. Then we both turned our heads and looked at Benny Nubb, who was hardly even paying attention to the tapping. He was watching the three guinea pigs with a little smile on his face instead.

TAP TAP TAP... TAP TAP TAP!

"Oh my gosh," I whispered. "Oh. My. Gosh. Max?"

TAP TAP TAP... TAP TAP TAP!
TAP TAP TAP... TAP TAP TAP!
TAP TAP TAP... TAP TAP TAP!
TAP TAP TAP... TAP TAP TAP!

Benny noticed that we were looking at him and said, "What?" Then he looked around at all of us. "What're you all looking at me for? What's that sound?"

Chapter Twenty
The mystery is solved

Benny Nubb stood very still, listening to the taps amid the wheeking and whooping that had started up again.

TAP TAP TAP . . . TAP TAP TAP!

TAP TAP TAP TAP TAP TAP! TAP TAP TAP TAP TAP TAP!

Those extra taps made me shivery, and it didn't help that the guys had turned their noise up another few notches.

"*EEEEEOOOOOEEEEEOOOOO!! EEEEEOOOOOEEEEEOOOOO!!*"

"*Wheek!! Wheek!! Wheek!! Wheek!! Wheek!! Wheek!!*"

Little Linny whooped pretty loudly too, catching the nerves from her new friends.

TAP TAP TAP TAP TAP TAP! TAP TAP TAP TAP TAP TAP!

Max said, "Holy cow!" about the guinea pig ruckus, then he picked up Teddy. "It's okay, buddy," he said. "Chill out, dude. It's just noise. Nothing to worry about."

TAP TAP TAP TAP TAP TAP! TAP TAP TAP TAP TAP TAP!

"I'll take her." Benny Nubb scooped Linny up, then stood there, still listening. "Shh," he said to her in a nice voice I could hardly believe came out of his mouth. "It's okay, Linny."

TAP TAP TAP TAP TAP TAP! TAP TAP TAP TAP TAP TAP!

Sophie and Max worked hard to calm down Teddy and noisy siren Pip.

TAP TAP TAP TAP TAP TAP! TAP TAP TAP TAP TAP TAP!

Benny Nubb headed right for the living room. "I think I know what it is," he said.

I followed him. "How could you . . . ?" I stopped myself from being upset by those words. Whatever it was, it wasn't him, and I had to be fair. "What?" I asked instead.

He didn't answer me. "It's okay, Linny, don't be scared."

TAP TAP TAP TAP TAP TAP! TAP TAP TAP TAP TAP TAP! TAP TAP! TAP TAP TAP!

I watched him walk slowly up to the windows. "What?" I whispered. "What do you think it is?"

He peeked around the edge of the curtain, but didn't move it, then pointed to the glowing red bird decoration thing.

I shook my head, disappointed. "That thing doesn't make noises. It's plastic or something. I think it's lit up from getting sunlight during the day and then. . . ."

TAP TAP TAP! TAP TAP TAP TAP TAP TAP! TAP TAP TAP TAP TAP TAP!

I jumped. I really wished I hadn't because it made him grin at me.
TAP TAP TAP TAP TAP TAP! TAP TAP TAP TAP TAP TAP!
He peeked between the curtain and the window again, then waved me over. "I know it isn't that thing. I was right. Look for yourself."
"Right about what?"
TAP TAP TAP!
I got close enough to look . . .
TAP TAP TAP TAP TAP TAP! TAP TAP TAP TAP TAP TAP!
. . . but backed up a bit when that happened. That made him grin again.
"It's nothing to be afraid of," he said, but not in the mean way I would have expected. "Come on, take a look. Don't move the curtain."
TAP TAP TAP TAP TAP TAP!!
I looked again.
"It's a cardinal," he said as my eyes found a pretty red bird — a real one — tapping his beak against the window, right where the glowing red bird decoration was hanging.
TAP TAP TAP . . . TAP TAP TAP!
TAP TAP TAP . . . TAP TAP TAP!
"You have got to be kidding me," I murmured. "A bird?"
"He likes that pretend bird in the window," Benny explained. "He's trying to get at it. That's all. Or else he doesn't like it and he's trying to scare it off."
I felt my mouth drop open and stay that way. "A bird," I finally said. "It's been a bird, all this time? Night and day? For hours?"

Benny Nubb shrugged. "They do that," he said. "Guess it likes or hates that glowing thing, so it didn't only do it at night."

"How in the world did you . . . could you . . . ?"

"Grandpa Nubb," he said. "He likes birds kind of a lot. There was one for a long time, like, totally attacking his window, and his car mirror, too."

"I can't believe this." I shook my head. "I never would've thought of that." Of course I wouldn't have, because I had thought it had been him all along, so I hadn't thought of anything else. "Sorry." The apologizing was really hard, and I had to stop for a second and get up my courage again. "I thought it was you."

His eyes narrowed up.

"Sorry," I said again.

It was quiet for a zillion years after I said that. Well, except for that crazy tapping cardinal.

Finally, he said, "Okay," and shrugged. Then he said, "Guess we're even, then."

And I said, "Maybe."

He grinned at me, then opened up the curtain. A flash of red bird disappeared into the night and Benny Nubb headed for the kitchen. "Are we gonna take pictures of these guinea pigs now, or what?"

Chapter Twenty-one
Play it again, Max

"Oh, yes! Redbirds will do that!" Grandma Rose nodded her head around at the other grandmas, who all agreed with her. "They don't like to have their territory invaded. No sir, they do not!"

I thought of Teddy's "carrot-ory" and smiled.

"One male to a house!" Grandma Pearl giggled.

"I've seen more than one boy cardinal at the feeder," someone else said, "but they do spar. Oh yes, they do!"

"I had no idea," I sighed. "I never thought about a bird. Not even for one second. Even though I have one. And there are all those awesome keets over there." I pointed toward the mega-parakeet area in the room, where at least twenty were chirping away.

Every single grandma in my club had heard of or seen a cardinal tapping on a window, and the stories went on and on.

If only I had had a Grandma Club meeting on Monday!

But, on the other hand, the sympathy for my tough week went on and on too. And they all really appreciated the cards (even though they were just copies this time), the cookies, and Max's video of my State Fair presentation.

Yep, Max videotaped the whole thing and brought it to Shady Acres. Is that a great idea, or what?

"Let's see the Molly Show again!" Grandma Lucy clapped her hands together. "Please? I think we would all love to see it again!"

There were lots of yeses about that. Max stopped putting away his computer and looked at Mom who said, "Sure. Why not?"

I pulled up a chair between two of my grandmas who I hadn't sat by yet, and we watched together.

The video started with a quick trip through the gym so we got to see all of the states, even the show-offs on either side of me. Max did not spend any extra time on any state, except for Wyoming (because Hannah and Kaylie were waving like crazy and giggling a lot). Then the camera stayed on New Hampshire.

"Tell us a little about your state, Molly," said a judge in a fancy suit. *"Tell us about the history of New Hampshire."*

"My partner, Nora, is actually going to do that part on the computer," said the me in the video. "Take it away, Nora!"

There was blankness for a few seconds, then a close-up of Max's computer, which was sitting on the project table. Then there was Nora Sutter, on the screen, wearing her matching purple T-shirt and headband.

"Max, pause it, please! I want to explain this part to the grandmas," I said. "Max went to my friend Nora's house this morning and made a video of her presentation. Isn't that a great idea?" All the grandmas clapped. "She was sick yesterday, so she would've missed the whole fair. She's fine today, though. Just a little tired."

Max got a little embarrassed from all the clapping and started up the video again.

The camera zoomed in on Nora's face so everyone could see her New Hampshire headband. *"And so, New Hampshire became our ninth state on June 21, 1788. Thanks for listening! And now, back to Molly!"* Nora smiled real big so we could see her red, white, and blue braces bands.

The grandmas clapped for Nora as the camera pulled back again, zooming in on the project board and the guinea pig pictures.

"Is that Pip, Molly?" Grandma Rose giggled.

"Yep! And Teddy is coming up, too," I said. "Keep watching!"

The picture of Pip was taking up the whole screen, with antlers on his adorable little head, dressed up as the state animal (the white tailed deer.)

Now the camera focused on Teddy, with a pumpkin hat, being the state fruit.

Linny, wearing a hat covered in purple lilacs, was next.

"Is that Nora's guinea pig?" someone asked.

"No, Grandma, that is the guinea pig Benny Nubb brought over."

"The boy who solved the cardinal mystery?" Grandma Helen asked.

I felt my face scrunch up a bit about that, but smoothed it out again. "Yes," I said. "And that guinea pig lives with his cousin. He is watching her for the weekend, which is very nice of him."

Max zoomed in on the cookie map. There was my hand with Daddy's cool laser pointer, pointing to mountains and rivers and stuff. The grandmas got quiet and listened up, except for the ones who had been to New Hampshire and remembered those places. They had a lot of New Hampshire memories to share.

Next we were looking at the symbol cookie platter: pumpkins, birds, deer (actually Christmas cookie reindeer, but who was going to know?), purple flower bouquets that were supposed to be lilacs, and plain old squares frosted in light gray (for granite). *"Feel free to enjoy a cookie before you go,"* I said on the TV. "You too, grandmas!" I said in real life. "They're really good. Trust me, I tried a few."

"But Molly, the cookies are so lovely!" Grandma Rose said. "Much too pretty to eat!"

"No they're not, Grandma! Dig in!" I said. "How about if next time I visit, I bring more? But I won't make 'em too pretty, okay?"

"Who's that, now?" Grandma Helen asked, pointing at the TV screen. She had missed the video the first time around because her daughter was visiting. (Barbara took one look at Teddy and Pip on the screen and wheeled her mom right out of the rec room! Believe me, those feelings are mutual! A Shady Acres helper led Grandma Helen back later.)

Anyway, it was Benny Nubb who she saw on the screen. He was grabbing a cookie, of course, and peeking sideways back into the camera. *"Hi, Molly Fisher!"* he yelled, then he grabbed that rubber newt, shoved it close to the camera so it looked like a big monster, crossed his eyes and chomped the cookie.

"*Uh, could you move a bit?*" said Max on TV. "*You're blocking the camera, dude.*"

Benny Nubb did a thumbs-up, then waved really fast and hard. He grabbed another cookie and disappeared.

As the clapping died down, I said, "Thanks, grandmas. But I could never have gotten the project done at all, and especially not as awesomely as it turned out, without tons of help. Especially from my cousin Max." I left my chair, ran toward him and hugged him so hard that he said, "Oomph!"

And that made me think that the oomph our project needed all along was Max.

More clapping.

"And I want to say one more humongous thank you to someone who isn't even here: Max's . . ." I looked right at him, then said, ". . . girlfriend. Sophie." That word made Max smile like crazy. "She had so many great ideas and was patient and nice, even when I was going cuckoo. She is one of my newest, bestest friends and will be the best teacher ever when she is done with college."

The grandmas thought it was wonderful that Max had such a nice girlfriend.

"But wait! There is something else to see! Max, we didn't play the . . . you know. The best part!"

"Oh yeah."

"Grandmas, this is even more awesome than what you've already seen!" I said. "Most of you already know and love Teddy and Pip," I started. "Teddy is the bigger one and Pip the noisy little one," I said for new members. "And Linny is in this movie too. Honestly, grandmas? That little guinea pig really helped to break the ice that was all over me and Benny Nubb yesterday. Guinea pigs do that, you know." I caught my mom's eye. Even she was smiling.

More clapping, as well as agreeing. And asking when they could see Teddy and Pip again.

"I'll talk to Wally and Amelia about it. And now . . ." I said, nodding at Max, ". . . grandmas — and grandpas," I added, because some grandpas had joined us now, "Mom and Max and everyone else, get ready for the cutest, coolest thing ever! Introducing: three guinea pigs with New Hampshire style. By the way, this was Max's idea. He's an electronical-techno-master-genius." Clapping. "This video played on the table during the whole fair, except when I was talking to judges. And it was just as popular and exciting as those crazy gambling machines on either side of me."

The TV screen came to life, and three guinea pigs walked to the middle: Teddy, Pip, and Linny. They were wearing red, white, and blue party hats that said "I LOVE NH" on them.

The Shady Acres audience went cuckoo (of course, because everyone loves guinea pigs).

There was some cool camera stuff going on, so it looked like those three were marching around and turning in circles and stuff with the New Hampshire state song playing in the background. The hats changed into different symbols, and there were close-ups and words on the bottom of the screen about the symbol.

When a potato (the state vegetable) popped into sight — an actual potato from Amelia's house — Pip sniffed at it, shook his head, and walked away. That made everyone giggle.

In the next scene, all three guinea pigs were happily eating parsley.

Of course, the last part was the coolest. Pip, center stage, singing his New Hampshire song.

New Hampshire is good.
Live there we all should.
Houses made of wood.
New Hampshire is good!

Finch birds in trees.
Lilacs in the breeze.
Live, live free!
New Hampshire is good!

Pumpkins, lady bugs.
Ski and ski and ski.
Live, live free!
New Hampshire is good!

Granite is the thing.
Deers are frolicking.
Guinea pigs are king!
New Hampshire is good!

Only a few watchers knew that he was really singing and it wasn't just a speeded-up human's voice. Max's rock and rolling background music made it extra cool. Trust me, no one loves this part more than Pip, the rock star.

In the background, Teddy and Linny popped in and out wearing symbol hats as he sang about them.

The final scene of that video was three guinea pigs with signs in front of them that said: VOTE FOR, NEW, and HAMPSHIRE. They were in the wrong order at first — HAMPSHIRE, NEW, VOTE FOR — and they switched places in a fast and funny way until the order was right.

The whole entire State Fair audience had stopped by (more than once) to see that video. Even the fifth grade boys. (Especially Benny Nubb. He probably stopped by four or five times.)

Chapter Twenty-two
Tweets is a genius

"I need to go to bed now," I yawned. "Good night, best friend Nora. I'm glad you feel better."

"Good night, best friend Molly. And hey, thanks for doing so much work on the project when I was sick. And, um, Molly?"

"Yeah?"

"I'm really sorry I was such a grouch before. Really sorry. Like, double-triple-quadruple —"

"Aw, it's okay. I mean, that stuff happens to everyone. I was a grouch too. I mean, on Thursday afternoon."

"It was really fun making the video and stuff." Nora yawned, too. "I can't believe Benny Nubb likes guinea pigs and that he helped you solve the mystery! What a weirdo day, huh?"

"The weirdo-est." I yawned again. I couldn't seem to stop yawning. "If you feel up to it, I'll see you tomorrow, okay?"

"I already feel better. Maybe we can make hats for Peanut and Coco and do a video! Do you think Max would help us?"

"He's coming over for dinner. I'll ask him." I yawned again. "It's about time we got back to guinea pigs and away from New Hampshire."

Nora said, "No kidding."

Daddy tapped on the door and stepped into my room. "Hi, sweetheart."

"Hi."

He fingered the blue ribbon that was hanging from my bed post, then sat next to me. "You made it."

"Yeah."

I hugged him tight, then let him hold on to me for a long while. "I feel like a pile of exhaustion, Daddy," I said.

"You were a trooper."

"Not really."

"I'm sorry Mom and I had to desert you when you needed us most."

"I know. But it worked out okay. I mean, in the end. Don't feel bad, Daddy. There'll be a next time."

I could feel him smiling. "Well? Was I right about Benny Nubb?"

"What do you mean?" I looked up at him. "Right about what?"

"That you'd end up being friends?"

I shook my head and his eyebrows went up a notch.

"Well, not all the way right. Maybe about eighty-seven percent right." I smiled.

"Eighty-seven? Not even a rounded-up ninety, huh?"

"I don't think you could call what we are 'friends,' but we are not enemies anymore. I think I understand him a little more, too."

"A step in the right direction."

"Yeah. But he's still a fifth-grade boy."

"Ah. Right."

"Mom was right about Sophie, though — one hundred percent right. Sorry, Daddy, Mom gets the purple ribbon about that." I grinned at his pouty lip. "I have the most awesome family ever," I sighed. "And the best friends, and guinea pigs. Do you believe how cool that video was? And Pip's song? The kids were going cuckoo for it, Daddy! That's one thing *I* was right about one hundred percent: guinea pigs make everything better."

"Know what else?" Daddy said.

"What else?"

"I'm proud of you, Molly," Daddy said, then kissed my forehead. "Real proud."

"Even though I didn't get the purple ribbon?"

Daddy did a little frown like he was thinking about that, then it turned into a smile and he tapped on my nose and said, "Of course."

"Oh my gosh." My eyes flew open really wide. "Oh my gosh!" I said again, really loud. "Tweets!"

"What about him? He's fine – he's sleeping."

"Daddy! Tweets is a genius!" Then I ran out of my room, leaving a confused Daddy alone on my bed.

Tweets was asleep with his little yellow-and-green head under a wing.

"Tweets?" I whispered. "Tweets?"

The head popped out from under the wing, and he stretched out a little leg before he hopped to where I had my face pressed against the cage bars. He tilted his head at me.

"You were right. You knew all along and kept telling me and telling me. There never was a mystery."

Tweets tilted his head the other way.

"You were right, sweetie."

"*Birdie,*" Tweets said quietly.

"Yeah. I'm sorry I didn't listen or figure it out. You are a genius." I gave him a kiss through the bars.

"*Hello.*"

"Hi."

"*Pretty.*"

I smiled at him. "I love you. You can go back to sleep now. Sorry I woke you up."

Tweets hopped back to his sleeping place.

And then — even though I can't really be sure of it because I was so sleepy — I think he said, very quietly:

"*. . . Love you.*"

Epilogue

"Wally, that girl guinea pig called Linny said to us that we were not right, or possibly that we are wrong, about monsters doing tapping," Teddy said. "She says to us that there are no monsters and we are being silly."

"NO GOOD! SHE WAS WRONG! SHE CALLED US SILLIES!"

"But, fellows —" Wally began.

"She says to us that Nubb is okay. He is a friend. But her best friend is a Nubb girl called Lizzie. She is missing that girl very much," Teddy interrupted.

"NUBB, NUBB, NUBB! BLUB, BLUB, BLUB! SO MANY NUBBS!"

"Boys, it sounds to me like Miss Linny was absolutely correct," Wally said.

"*OBJECTION!*"

"Nope."

"The tapping noises were made by a confused bird, not by monsters."

"*SHE WAS NOT CORRECT! DO NOT SAY THAT THING, WALLY! SHE WAS BOSSY AND WRONG!*"

"What precisely was she wrong about, Pippen?"

"*ABOUT... THINGS! PRECISELY!*"

I smiled at Wally, then we shook our heads and decided it was better not to argue.

"So much excitement on Taylor Drive, and I missed it all," Wally said with his warm chuckle. He scratched Teddy behind the ears until he purred, then switched to jealous-siren Pip.

"If you were here, you would've figured it all out about that bird." I said.

"Possibly, but possibly not," Wally said kindly.

"*Hi, Amelia!*" Teddy's head popped up. "*Veggies? For me?*"

"*AND ME! DO NOT FORGET ABOUT THIS ROCK STAR!*"

"Yes, boys, veggies for both of you." Amelia set bowls in the front yard of the big house that Teddy and Pip had moved back into. "How is Eli doing, darling?" she asked Wally.

"That's your friend, right? The one who was sick?" I asked.

"Yes, indeed. He is quite well, I am pleased to say," Wally said as he set both of the guinea pigs on the walkway behind the couch.

They waddled to the house for snacks, chattering away about Linny and how bossy (but cute) she was.

"Even after that lovely and nearly full night of sleep, I am still struggling to wrap my mind around all that went on," Amelia sighed. "Especially the fact that my funny little solar cardinal decoration was the direct cause of so much chaos."

"But nobody would think a thing like that," I said. "Or think that a bird would go so cuckoo over it."

"Thank you, Molly." Amelia smiled.

"You found that in Portland — is that right?" Wally asked.

"In that gift ship I mentioned, yes. I thought it was so lovely and funny, and that the boys would enjoy seeing the bird light up at night."

"*Funny and not funny, Amelia,*" Teddy said with a mouth full of lettuce.

"*TEE HEE AND NOT TEE HEE! BEST OF TIMES, WORST OF TIMES!*"

Amelia sighed and we all turned to look at the plastic bird, now hanging far away from the window.

"It is a very lovely thing, my darling," Wally said kindly. "And yes, funny, too. Perhaps once our jealous cardinal friend comes to his senses, we can —"

"Oh, it doesn't matter. It can stay right there." Amelia sat beside him on the couch and took his hand. "What matters is that now you are home, and all is well. And," she looked from Teddy to Pip, "these two can rest easy and enjoy this lovely, safe, not-haunted house once again."

Teddy and Pip quietly munched veggies, not saying a thing.

"The Nubbs have agreed to keep a closer eye on their dog," Amelia said. "Apparently he has been roaming, sometimes at night, and has ended up in our front garden. According to Linny the guinea pig, translated by these two, the dog enjoyed watching the cardinal. And, amazingly, he stood and watched, not making a sound or scaring him off."

"Linny can talk to dogs?" I asked.

"*Possibly, or maybe not,*" Teddy shook his head. "*She says to us that it is not monster feet we are hearing, but instead, dog feet.*"

"The crunching was Benny Nubb's dog walking on rocks?"

"Yes, I believe so," Amelia said. "It makes sense."

"*Some sense and no sense.*"

"CRUNCHY MONSTER FEET," Pip mumbled. "*I WAS NOT WRONG. PIP IS A ROCK STAR.*"

"Well, Molly? Have we had enough adventure for a while?" Amelia asked.

"Yes," I said with a sigh. "I am ready for a long, not-exciting summer."

"I, Miss Molly, am with you on that one," Wally said.

"As am I." Amelia smiled, then she leaned forward and adjusted the statue of the girl with the umbrella on the coffee table. "As am I."

THE END

PIP'S HIT SINGLES

TAPPING

Tap tap tap! I hear it and dread.
Tap-ping scares me out of my head!
Tap tap tap! It comes in the night.
Tap tap tap! It gives us a fright!
Tap tap, clickety fingers, I say.
The tapping is monsters, and we need to move away!

MOLLY JANE WILL SAVE THE DAY

If a day needs saving,
Molly Jane will do it!
If a day needs saving,
She is the one!
If a day needs saving,
Molly Jane will do it!
As soon as we see . . . the sun!

HAUNTED HOUSES STINK

Haunted houses stink.
It's not like you think.
Scared to take a drink,
Or be too close to the sink.

Haunted . . . houses . . . STINK!

NUBB
Neigh-bor boy of Nubb
(Blub-blub-blub),
LEAVE. US. ALONE!
Neigh-bor boy of Nubb
(Blub-blub-blub),
LEAVE! US! ALONE!!!!

SOPHIE
Sophie will come,
Monsters will go.
Don't ask how,
'Cuz I just know!

RAIN
Rain rain rain rain,
Rain-rain — GO AWAY!
Rain rain rain rain,
I don't like you so GO AWAY!

Boom boom boom boom!
Boom-boom — STOP THE BOOM!
Boom boom boom boom!

Lisa Maddock

I don't like you so GO TO YOUR ROOM!

Click click click click,
Monsters, GO AWAY!
Click click click click,
I don't like you so STAY AWAY!

NEW HAMPSHIRE
New Hampshire is good.
Live there we all should.
Houses made of wood.
New Hampshire is good!

Finch birds in trees.
Lilacs in the breeze.
Live, live free!
New Hampshire is good!

Pumpkins, lady bugs.
Ski and ski and ski.
Live, live free!
New Hampshire is good!

Granite is the thing.
Deers are frolicking.

Guinea pigs are king!
New Hampshire is good!

OOMPH *(A bonus hit single!)*
Words don't rhyme with oomph.
(UH UH!)
It's a silly, silly thing.
(NO GOOD!)
But Molly Jane wants some anyway.
(WHY?!)
For her State Fair-project-thing.
(THAT'S WHY!)

NOSES *(Another bonus hit single!)*
Noses are funny, they make me tee hee
Everybody has one, even Teddy and me!
They make funny noises like whistle and snort
Some are real long and some very short!

Noses are good for smelling and stuff
Not having one wouldn't be enough!
A face with no nose would look silly I say
Thanks for the nose on my face today!

BEST FRIENDS CLUB
(as of December 1, 2013)

HUMANS
Wally • Amelia • Molly Jane • Dad Dan • Bill • Lisa • Allison • Mia • Alexandria • Nancy • Jennah • Terri • Bella • Sophia • Sam • Cally • Jessamine • Jake • Mackenzie • Seth • Alexandra • Chantal • Isaac • Goldie • Ruth • Rose • Lenny • Annie • Benjamin • Ryann • Emilyn • Hannah • Eric • Aidan • Amber • Grace • Chloe • Vahishta • Lily • MollyAnn • Darren • Dylan • Logan • Abby • Bella • Mckayla • Hannah • Maggie • Patterson's First Grade Class • Ruth • Sofie • Calli • Lizzie • Kayla • Kaylee • Joanna (and family) • Gwen • Ally • Alexandrea • Vahishta

GUINEA PIGS
Teddy • Pip • Maggie • Peanut • Mimi • Miranda • Coco • Magic • Muffin • Nugget • Squeak • Hershey • Butterscotch • Ormsby • Pedrosa • Chestnut • Mocha • Scamp • LiL Betty • Angelstunky • Squeakersiren • Gizmo • Princess • Pearl • Cinnamon • Sugar • Fuzzy • Spice • Peruvian • Linniea Serena Silkie • Fuzzcake • Pipsqueak • Molly • Rosie • Babooshka • Little Fussy • S'mores • Sparkle • Bevo • Ranger • Oreo • Freckles • Cappy • Ginger • Pumpkin • Twinkie • Ginger • Piko • Lola • Lotta • Butterscotch • Stanley • Mr. Pickles • Oreo • Chewy • Stripes • Snowball • Jilly Boo • PeeWee • Pipsqueak • Teddy • Dalmation • Skippy • Linny • Snickers • Romeo • Juliet • Alexander • Angel • Chester (Mr. Awesome) • Squeakers • Princess • Junior • Marshmallow •Mischief • Herb • Chanel • Magic • Cream • Willow • Zuna • Sadie • Autumn • Malena • Swift Tom • Caramel Chip • Rosie • Fluffy • Cupcake

Introducing Nubb Trouble special guest:

Lizzie's guinea pig Linny!

For more fun with Teddy and Pip, go to
www.teddyandpip.com

Made in the USA
Las Vegas, NV
16 December 2021